THE ULVERSCROFT FOUNDATION,
c/o The Royal Australian and New Zealand
College of Ophthalmologists,
94-98 Chalmers Street, Surry Hills,
N.S.W. 2010, Australia

John Dean is an award-winning journalist from Darlington, Co. Durham. He has twice been named North-East Freelance Journalist of the Year and also Environmental Reporter of the Year. He has contributed to papers such as *The Sunday Telegraph*, *The Sunday Times* and *The Daily Express*.

THE SECRETS MAN

When DCI John Blizzard visits a friend in hospital, he is intrigued when an elderly villain in the next bed reveals much about Hafton's criminal gangs. These revelations attract a series of sinister characters to the ward. Blizzard wonders if they are seeking to silence the old man, but fellow detectives believe that the pensioner is suffering from dementia. It's only when people start dying that his colleagues take the DCI seriously. Blizzard faces a race against time to save lives, and must face a part of his past he's tried to forget — and with the one man he fears.

JOHN DEAN

THE
SECRETS
MAN

Complete and Unabridged

ULVERSCROFT
Leicester

First published in Great Britain in 2011 by
Robert Hale
London

First Large Print Edition
published 2012
by arrangement with
Robert Hale
London

British Library CIP Data

Dean, John, *1961* –
The secrets man.
1. Blizzard, John (Fictitious character)- -Fiction. 2. Police
- -England- -Fiction. 3. Gangs- -Fiction. 4. Murder- -
Investigation- -Fiction. 5. Detective and mystery stories.
6. Large type books.
I. Title
823.9′2–dc23

ISBN 978–1–4448–1210–7

Published by
F. A. Thorpe (Publishing)
Anstey, Leicestershire

Set by Words & Graphics Ltd.
Anstey, Leicestershire
Printed and bound in Great Britain by
T. J. International Ltd., Padstow, Cornwall

1

It was shortly before midnight when an inebriated Des Fairley finally staggered from the warmth of the back-street public house into the sharp chill of a winter's night. He had been ensconced in The Kestrel since just after lunchtime and had consumed more pints than he could count, drinking solidly, one glass emptied, another one immediately started as he celebrated his fortieth birthday. It had been a proper session and during the afternoon and evening, more and more of his associates had drifted into the pub to join him, until by mid-evening it was packed with people he knew. Des Fairley had been in his element, holding court, sometimes loud and funny, sometimes conspiratorial, often controversial, always the centre of attention, and relishing every minute as people bought him drinks, pints at first, shorts later. Brash and arrogant, Fairley was enjoying himself, loved being a somebody in the criminal fraternity, loved the kudos that came with being part of Morrie Raynor's inner circle. That counted for a lot in the northern city of Hafton. It counted for everything in Des Fairley's world.

As the evening wore on, the atmosphere changed in the pub as, his tongue loosened by alcohol, Fairley started to utter derogatory comments about Raynor. One by one, his uneasy drinking companions drifted away to join other conversations, eager to distance themselves from Des Fairley when he was in this mood. Even Harry Josephs and Geoff Bates, good friends as they were, eventually made themselves scarce. If it came to taking sides, everyone knew that you wanted to be full square behind Morrie Raynor. No one bad-mouthed him. At one point, Josephs had sidled across to his friend and hissed, 'Will you quiet your mouth, daft lad?' but Fairley ignored him. Harry Josephs gave a shrug, muttered 'Your funeral' and turned away.

By eleven, Josephs and Bates had gone and as the bar gradually emptied, one or two others tried to remonstrate with Fairley but, deep in his cups by now, he shrugged them all off, seemingly impervious to the drinkers shooting increasingly uncomfortable looks towards the door, fearful lest Morrie Raynor should appear. The thought of his thin smile was enough to strike fear into otherwise stout souls.

By the end of the night, only a few brave men remained in the bar and Des Fairley had lapsed into drunken silence. Now, the stoppy-back at an end, he was standing in the doorway to the pub, swaying slightly and fumbling with the buttons on his camel-hair coat, eventually cursing and giving up, defeated by a combination of alcohol and the biting cold. A couple of men emerged from the lounge and brushed roughly past him, muttering hurried goodbyes but keen not to be seen talking to him. Fairley watched them make their way rapidly down the street and disappear around the corner, grateful to be well away from The Kestrel.

'Cowards,' he slurred to himself. Drunk or not, he knew that no one wanted to be around him on a night like this.

But someone did.

As Fairley turned up his collar and stepped unsteadily out onto a pavement already glistening with gathering frost, he noticed for the first time the lone figure standing at the end of the street, surveying him silently. Fairley felt the first tug of fear as the man started to walk slowly towards him, his pace steady and unhurried. Fairley peered closer, sensing that he recognized him but unable to make out the features at that distance.

'You after me, pal?' he slurred loudly.

There was the sound of a slamming door and, glancing behind him, Fairley saw that the pub had been plunged into darkness. The stranger said nothing but kept walking until he was just twenty feet away, where he stopped under a street light. Fairley gazed on the face.

'No,' he breathed. 'No, surely no.'

Turning, Fairley started to run. At the end of the street, and breathing hard, he dared to look back and saw that the man had not moved but was watching him go. Fairley breathed a sigh of relief then gave a light laugh. OK, he was not stupid, he knew he had been shooting his mouth off back there in the bar, but he also knew that Morrie Raynor would understand. Morrie Raynor trusted him, he and Morrie Raynor had something special going, everyone knew that. Right-hand man, that was the phrase Morrie used about him. Yes, Des Fairley was a somebody in this city.

The shot dropped Des Fairley where he stood.

2

A weary John Blizzard reached the top stair and paused to catch his breath, leaning against the wall and listening gloomily to the wheezing sound emanating from his lungs. Ever since he had been visiting Hafton General Hospital to see George Moore, Blizzard had been taking the stairs, driven by the need to lose weight. Such sentiments did not come naturally to the detective chief inspector but he realized that greater forces than he were at work, his health campaign driven by the constant memos from head-quarters. Blizzard usually ignored memos, but he knew that the new breed of top brass frowned on unfit police officers. He had already seen one or two old friends pensioned off because of their inability to meet the chief constable's exacting standards, and the inspector reckoned that eschewing the lift in favour of the hospital stairs, all 127 of them, might help. If it did not kill him first, he thought darkly, as he felt his breathing slow to normal and his pulse stop racing.

He caught sight of himself in the full-length mirror on the far wall and paused for a few moments to survey what he saw. He had been doing it more and more since the hospital visits had started; something about a sense of his own mortality, he imagined, that and murmurings about cost-cuttings within the force and early retirement being offered to longer serving officers. What Blizzard saw was someone in his late forties, a broad-chested man slightly heavier than someone of five foot ten inches should be, a man wearing his customary dark suit beneath a black coat flecked with snow, his red tie dangling loosely at its pre-ordained half-mast position and his hair tousled as ever. Somehow he looked older, Blizzard thought; there was no doubt about the emerging wrinkles and flecks of grey hair cruelly exposed in the harsh glare of the strip light. God, how he hated hospitals and how he loathed the bright spark who had decided that it would be a good idea to hang a mirror at the top of the stairs.

Blizzard glanced at his watch — 6.55 p.m. it said — and mopped the sweat away from his brow with a handkerchief before carrying out a cursory straightening of his tie and running a hand through his hair, after which he pulled open the door and walked out onto the fourth floor. He headed along the corridor in the direction of Ward 46. He had been coming to the hospital for almost two months now — at least once a week, sometimes twice, always after work — and had found his mood darkening day by day, not helped by the relentless snow and ice that had held Hafton in its grip for weeks. He was, however, determined to keep making the journey because his friendship with George went back more than twenty years.

The relationship had started in Blizzard's early days in CID over in Hafton's Eastern Division. George Moore was a detective chief inspector at the time, the older man teaching the eager young officer so many of the lessons that had remained with him down the years. After eighteen months, Blizzard was promoted and moved across the city to work in Western Division, eventually rising to become head of CID. The friends never worked together again, although they did remain in contact, the younger man occasionally ringing George for advice usually imparted over a pint. Blizzard had always been grateful for the help and felt that it was a debt he still owed George Moore; it was a debt that kept him heading to the hospital during these dark nights of winter.

As he walked down the corridor, and heard another wheeze from his chest, Blizzard glanced at the posters lining the walls. *Are you drinking too much? Are you taking enough exercise? Are you loving your heart enough?*

'Just leave me alone,' he muttered.

Reaching the double doors at the far end of the corridor, he pressed the security button and waited for the click which would admit him to Ward 46. Walking through, he made his way down the corridor, nodding at a couple of the nurses who had become like old friends during his visits but whose names he still did not know. George Moore, who was in his early eighties and lived in a warden-controlled housing complex on the east side, had been taken into the hospital after being struck down with an infection in mid-December. Although he had finally started to show signs of rallying, there were still setbacks and his condition changed from day to day; good days when he was awake and in control of his senses, when he would talk rationally and affectionately to the inspector, and others when he would not recognize his old friend and instead would drift in and out of sleep, illness turning his few words into confused ramblings which made no sense. Blizzard paused before walking into the side ward, wondering as ever which version would confront him tonight.

★ ★ ★

Alex Mather glanced at his watch — 6.55.

'He's late,' he murmured.

The east-side vice squad detective was standing in the lee of a wall on the edge of a playing field, stamping his feet to keep warm in the plunging evening temperatures. Listening to the distant hum of traffic on the main road and, glancing to his right towards the lights on in the tower blocks of the nearby housing estate, Mather felt strangely divorced from the rest of the world. Disconnected. He liked the feeling, always had. Had never felt like he belonged. He tensed at the sound of approach, relaxing when he saw a familiar figure emerge through the gloom.

'You're late,' said the undercover officer bluntly. 'If I say quarter to, I mean it.'

'Sorry.' The man did not sound it.

'What you got for me?'

'Some useful stuff on that place down Renard Street. Definitely a brothel. Two blokes from Malaysia and half-a-dozen girls. Chinese or something.'

'Got any names?'

'Ping Pong or summat.'

'Your commitment to international understanding is commendable,' murmured Mather. 'They there now?'

'Good chance. Where's me money?'

'Not sure you deserve it,' said Mather,

'without any names.'

'Might have something else for you,' said the man. 'Won't get it until tomorrow, mind.'

'What is it?'

'That kid over on the west side, the one that got herself drugged up.'

'Lorraine Hennessey — what of her?' asked Mather.

'Might be about that.'

'Ring me when you know.' Mather turned to go.

'Can't I have something now?' The voice sounded plaintive.

Mather turned back and surveyed the man, noting that he was trembling slightly. He guessed it was nothing to do with the cold.

'When did you last score?' asked the detective.

'This morning.'

Mather reached into his trouser pocket and produced a couple of notes.

'Thanks,' said the man. He hesitated then said, 'You know a cop called Blizzard?'

'Might do. Why?'

'Just wondered.'

Before Mather could ask him what he meant, the informant had gone. Mather watched him walk down the path and disappear into the darkness. As ever, he wondered if it would be the last time he saw him. And this time, he wondered why he had mentioned John Blizzard. Mather pondered the comment, wondered whether or not to contact his old friend. He dismissed the idea. What would he tell him?

3

Blizzard walked into the side room and headed for the bed nearest the window, to where George lay, eyes closed, cheeks sunken, breathing shallow. Moving quietly so as not to waken his slumbering friend, Blizzard pulled up a chair, pausing for a few moments to stare out of the window, letting his gaze roam across the snow-covered roofs of the Victorian terraced houses and the illuminated office blocks in the nearby city centre. As so often, Blizzard played the game of trying to identify the larger buildings, marvelling as ever that such huge structures could have passed him by even though he had worked in the city for his entire career and lived there since he was a teenager. As ever, he failed dismally to put names to any of the buildings and resolved to discover what they were once he had departed. He knew that he never would get round to it. It was, he had always thought, the nature of hospitals, that promises made within their walls were rarely made good on the outside.

Turning from the window, he sat down, wriggled out of his coat and glanced around the dimly-lit room. One of the beds was empty but the other four were occupied. Two of the old men had visitors, relatives hunched over and speaking in quiet tones, as if they felt that the dim light forbade them raising their voices. The man asleep in the next bed to George Moore had no one with him. Blizzard had not seen him before; they seemed to come and go from the ward at a bewildering rate, thought the inspector. He often wondered where they went. Home? Another ward? Mortuary? He did not know and he never asked. As the man stirred and muttered something, Blizzard glanced at the name scrawled on the whiteboard behind his bed. Josephs. Harry Josephs. Blizzard looked closer at the man. Memories stirred.

The inspector's reverie was disturbed by the approach of a young nurse who nodded at George.

'We had him sitting up today,' she said. 'Even had him walking a few paces.'

'How long's he been asleep?'

'An hour or so. I think we wore him out.'

'He'd have enjoyed it, though,' said Blizzard, with a smile. 'He always did have a thing for women in uniform.'

'Don't they all,' she grinned.

'This chap?' asked Blizzard, gesturing to Harry Josephs. 'When did he come in?'

'This afternoon. You know him?'

'No, just wondering.'

'Your friend seems to know him.'

'What makes you say that?'

'Seemed really agitated when he came in.' She lowered her voice. 'Look, between you and me, we gave George a little something to help him sleep. The last thing we want is him getting upset. They get agitated about all sorts of strange things when they're like this.'

She walked over to another of the beds and the inspector looked back at his friend. As ever in these situations, he wondered what to do; let him sleep or reach out and touch him on the wrist to wake him up. He sighed and allowed himself to recall happier times. Even two months previously, George had been fit and healthy, often to be seen striding purposefully through the town centre or enjoying a game of bowls with friends in the summer. Blizzard recalled the only time George persuaded him to try the game. It was a Saturday afternoon in July and Blizzard had been walking through the park with Fee when George shouted across at them from the green. Despite plenty of half-hearted protesting, Blizzard had reluctantly consented to send a bowl down. After it careered into the next game, wrecking what had been a tight end, the detective had announced his

14

immediate retirement, the comment banishing the frowns of irritation from the elderly women whose game he had disturbed. Blizzard smiled now at the memory; those carefree days of summer seemed a long time ago as snow flecked the hospital window.

George opened his eyes and gave a weak smile.

'Now then, John, lad,' he said. 'All right?'

'Yeah, George,' said the inspector, taking the old man's proffered hand, bony and mottled. 'You?'

'Yeah. Got something to tell you.' He tried to sit up. 'Something important.'

'Which is?'

Moore appeared not to have heard the question and closed his eyes. Twenty minutes later, his friend not having spoken again, Blizzard gently let go of the hand and stood up to go. As he did so, the old man in the next bed sat up.

'Please,' said Harry Josephs, 'please, will somebody help me?'

'Sorry, old son,' said Blizzard. 'I'm not a nurse.'

Josephs turned sunken eyes on him.

'Nobody ever helps me,' he said.

'I'm sure that's not true,' said Blizzard, putting the chair back and putting his coat on. 'My experience of the nurses here is that they do a superb job under very difficult — '

'Is that you, Des?' asked the man, looking closer and reaching out a clawed hand.

'Sorry again,' said the inspector, replacing the chair by the window.

'Just quiet your mouth, daft lad.'

Blizzard ignored the comment and started walking towards the door.

'Just quiet your mouth, I said,' hissed the man and something in the intensity of the voice made the inspector turn round; he noticed that the other visitors were watching as well. 'You don't know what you're saying, Des.'

'I told you, I'm not Des.'

'Well you just watch what you're saying,' said the man, a hint of alarm in his voice now. 'You know what Morrie will do if he hears you shooting your mouth off.'

'Morrie who?' said Blizzard sharply.

'Morrie who? he says,' said Josephs with a dry laugh, his wild eyes darting round the room. 'Listen to him.'

'Morrie Raynor?'

Josephs gave him a confused look.

'Morrie Raynor?' repeated the inspector. 'Do you mean Morrie Raynor?'

'Please,' said the old man, closing his eyes and lying down, appearing not to have heard the question. His voice was little more than a

16

whisper now. 'Please, will somebody help me?'

'Sad, isn't it?' said a grey-haired woman sitting at a nearby bed and holding the hand of another elderly man. 'That it should come to this.'

'Yeah,' murmured Blizzard, glancing at George, 'yeah, it is.'

'It your dad, luvvie?'

Blizzard shook his head.

'No,' he said. 'Just an old friend.'

The woman returned her attention to her sleeping husband and Blizzard looked at Harry Josephs again. The old man had slipped back into slumber, mouthing silent words. Blizzard glanced once more at the name on the whiteboard and frowned. With a thoughtful expression on his face, the inspector walked slowly out of the ward. Once out in the main corridor, the rumbling in his stomach reminded him that he had not eaten since lunchtime so he decided to make for the hospital's ground-floor restaurant. Ignoring the posters by the lifts, he headed back down the stairs.

When he reached the second floor, he looked up at the sign saying 'To Ward 23'. Blizzard sighed; he had walked past it many times in previous weeks; too many times. He followed the sign, reached the double doors

17

and pressed the ward's entry button. Once in, he took the first door on the left and walked into a semi-lit side room. Silently, he surveyed the young blonde woman lying in the only bed. Her eyes were closed and she was hooked up to life support machines.

'Sorry, pet,' murmured Blizzard. 'We've not served you well.'

'I'm sure that's not true, Chief Inspector,' said a voice and, startled, he turned to see one of the nurses entering the room. 'We have not seen you for a while. Has something happened?'

'No, just thought I would check up on her. Should have come earlier really.'

'Not sure what good it would have done. Most people in such cases only visit to make themselves feel better. Hardly ever see her dad these days.'

'No change in her condition then?'

'Nor, I fear, will there be now.' She gave a sad shake of the head. 'The consultants are holding a meeting in the next few days to decide what to do.'

'Might they turn her off?' said Blizzard, glancing towards the machines.

'There is only so much that the body can repair.'

'I'll take that as a yes.'

She did not reply and the two of them

stood and looked in silence at the young girl, her peaceful demeanour in stark contrast to the cataclysmic events that had overtaken her a year previously when she consumed the cocktail of drugs that had wreaked such damage on her organs.

'You're not the only one to have visited her, you know,' said the nurse. 'That young sergeant has been a couple of times. I forget his name, David something. Just had a baby.'

'Colley.'

'That's him. Nice young man.' The nurse looked back to the girl. 'He didn't seem to think you were any nearer to finding out who caused this. Is that so?'

'I am afraid it is.'

'I am sure you are doing your best.'

'It does not feel like it,' said the inspector, turning to leave the room. 'Goodnight, Nurse.'

'Goodnight, Chief Inspector.'

When Blizzard reached the ground floor, he made for the hospital café, which was virtually deserted save for a young couple in the corner, the woman wearing a dressing-gown and leaning across the table to hold the man's hand — she looked like she had been crying, he was close to tears as well — and on the other side of the room, a pale, middle-aged man who stared wordlessly into a cup of tea that looked as if it had long gone cold. Blizzard wondered what had befallen him to look so forlorn. It was what he always thought when he visited the place. So many stories. So many tragedies. Blizzard walked up to the counter where stood a young brunette in a green uniform. She gave him a bright smile. It was a smile that usually cheered the inspector's spirits — but not this time.

'You look down tonight,' she said. 'Is your friend bad?'

Blizzard hesitated.

'Sorry,' she said quickly. 'I shouldn't have asked.'

'It's all right, Amy. No, I've just been to see a seventeen-year-old girl who has been in a coma since September.'

'Lorraine Hennessey?'

'You know her?'

'We went to the same college. Really bright girl. Such a tragedy what happened to her.' She looked thoughtful. 'I guess we never know how things will end up — I mean, I never thought I would end up working behind the counter in a hospital café.'

'You're worth better than that,' said Blizzard; he had grown to like her over the weeks. 'Tell me, what kind of a person was Lorraine?'

'She was always really nice. The last person to try drugs, you'd imagine. Mind, we were never close so maybe I'm wrong.'

'It certainly came as a shock to her parents.'

'Her existence would have come as a shock to them.' She clapped a hand to her mouth. 'Sorry, uncalled for.'

'What made you say it?'

She paused.

'Off the record,' said Blizzard.

'Like I said, I did not know her that well but, from what I heard, her parents were more interested in their careers to take much notice of Lorraine, particularly her father.' She gave him an anxious look. 'But I should not really have said anything.'

'I'll not tell anyone.'

'Are you any closer to finding out who supplied her with the stuff?'

'A lot of dead-ends,' said Blizzard.

'I am sure you're doing your best.'

'You're the second person to have said that to me in the past ten minutes.'

'We must both be right then. Tea?' she asked.

'Please.'

'So how was your friend? George, isn't it?' asked the girl, busying herself at the machine.

'Not brilliant. He's very tired.' As he

watched Amy making the tea, Blizzard's mind went back to the strange encounter with Harry Josephs and the old man's words of warning. 'Maybe there comes a time when you just give up.'

He was surprised to hear the words coming out: he had no idea he had voiced his thoughts and he had no idea why he should confide in this young woman. She'd make a good counsellor, he thought. He'd said that to Colley several times over recent weeks. Perhaps he could recommend her to someone, thought Blizzard, get her out of this place. But he knew he wouldn't.

'That's a bit philosophical for this place,' she said, half turning as she filled the mug. 'Normally, it's what kind of cheese do we use with the macaroni?'

'Ignore me,' said Blizzard. 'This place does strange things to you.'

'Tell me about it,' she grinned, handing over his tea. 'So, what do you want tonight? I can do you some eggs? Not exactly cordon bleu but it fills a hole. If you're lucky, I might even do you an extra slice of toast.'

'Temptress,' said Blizzard, handing over a five pound note.

'I'll bring it over when it's ready.'

'Thank you,' said Blizzard and walked to one of the tables.

Sitting there in the sterilized, low-lit quiet of the café, the inspector stared into the middle distance, his mind coming back every time to Harry Joseph. And to Morrie Raynor. And to Lorraine Hennessey, lying peacefully in her hospital bed, the painful reminder of an investigation that had faltered. Ten minutes later, when Amy brought the eggs over, the detective had still not touched his drink. Remembering the man whose tea had gone cold, the inspector glanced round to see if he was still there, but Blizzard was now the only customer left. The inspector had never felt as desolate as he felt in that moment.

★ ★ ★

Up on Ward 23, the nurse stood at the entrance to the side room and looked sadly at the young girl.

'Goodnight, lovey,' she said. 'Sleep tight.'

And she closed the door.

★ ★ ★

Visiting time had finished on Ward 46 when three burly, bull-necked and grey-haired men arrived to find the door locked. They rattled it until it was opened by one of the young nurses.

'Will you be quiet?' said Alison Ramage. 'You'll disturb the patients.'

'We're here to see our mate,' said Geoff Bates, their leader.

'Visiting time is over.' She pointed to the clock on the wall. 'You'll have to come back tomorrow.'

'But we want to see him now.' The voice was harsh.

'Well, you can't — '

Bates pushed harder on the door, knocking Nurse Ramage aside, the young woman giving a cry as she hit her head on the wall. Ignoring her, the men marched down the corridor, looking in at each door, only to be confronted by a grim-faced Sister Maureen Cox, arms crossed, fire in her eyes.

'What the hell is happening here?' she said angrily.

'They barged me out of the way,' said the young nurse, running up behind the men, rubbing her injured cheek. 'I told them they could not get in, but they just — '

'Call Security,' said the sister, watching the nurse head for the telephone then returning her attention to the men, surveying them with a slight smile on her face. 'Come on, lads, don't you think that you're getting a bit old for this kind of behaviour?'

'We need to talk to our mate,' insisted

24

Bates. 'It's important.'

'He's far too ill to see anyone. Leave my ward, please.'

Bates glanced round and noticed the name Harry Josephs written on a board next to one of the doors.

'He in there?' he said.

'Get out of my ward, Geoff,' repeated the sister, stepping forward to block his way into the room, 'and take your cronies with you. The last thing Harry needs is the likes of you.'

The men turned at the sound of the main doors being pushed open as a couple of security guards appeared at the end of the corridor. Bates looked back at the resolute figure of Sister Cox.

'You'll regret this,' he said. 'You will fucking regret this, Maureen.'

Watching them stalk down the corridor and brush angrily past the security guards, Maureen Cox could feel the pounding of her heart.

4

Instead of heading home after leaving the hospital, Blizzard made the short journey to Abbey Road Police Station, his mind a whirl of thoughts as he guided his car through the snow flurries whipped ever sharper across the city streets. On the way, he had to slow down to allow an ambulance to pass, its siren blaring and light flashing. Arriving at Abbey Road, he parked his Ford Granada in the station car-park, turned his collar up against the chill wind and walked gingerly along the path to the back door, his feet slipping on ice that had not melted for days. Once inside the building, the inspector walked through deserted half-lit corridors, the silence and the solitude suiting the darkness of his mood, until he reached his office where he switched on the desk lamp, walked over to the corner of the room and flicked the kettle's switch.

As he waited for the kettle to boil, his hand resting on it to feel the welcome warmth, the inspector stared gloomily at the paperwork piled up in his in-tray. There had been little crime in Western Division for a couple of weeks — the inspector assumed that a combination of prolonged bad weather and post-Christmas blues was deterring even the villains — and the lull had allowed Blizzard to catch up with the bureaucratic tasks which he so loathed but from which he could not escape, try as he might. And he had tried. Oh, how he had tried. The detectives under his command had come to dread his arrival as the bored chief inspector meddled in matters in which he would normally have shown little interest, wandering into offices, idly picking up documents from desks and asking questions to which he did not really require answers.

Now, he reached over to his tray and picked up the top document. He could have sworn it was not there when he left to visit George: that's what happened these days, he thought sourly, turn your back for a moment and someone sneaks in and dumps more rubbish on your desk. It would be HR, he told himself, and wondered idly if they deliberately waited for him to go out before they did it. He resisted the temptation to walk out into the corridor to check if he could see someone's retreating back.

Blizzard replaced the paper in the tray, made the tea and sat down at the desk, listening to the snow blowing with increasing ferocity against the window. It felt strangely

27

comforting to be in the office after the impersonal corridors of the hospital. Blizzard had spent most of his career at Abbey Road and the place had come to feel like home. Constructed as a temporary measure in the 1960s, the single-storey station was still there three decades later, its corridors snaking in an octagonal-shape, the green paint on its prefabs peeling, the roof leaking and the heating system erratic. Sited in a middle-class residential area, the station was at the heart of Western Division; to its north, Victorian terraced houses virtually all now bedsits, to its east, the city centre and, fanning out to the west, run-down sixties council estates which eventually gave way to more affluent areas and the farming flatlands beyond Hafton's outer limits.

A short distance to the south of the station ran the River Haft, the banks of which had provided the backdrop for Blizzard's encounter with Morrie Raynor a decade previously, an encounter which the inspector recalled now. Blizzard knew that the words uttered by Harry Josephs were the ramblings of a mind disturbed by illness, but he could not help but feel that they held a truth of some kind if only he could fathom their meaning.

Cursing himself, Blizzard tried to think of something else before the showreel of that night down on the dockside started to play again, as it had done so many times before over recent months. The inspector had worked hard to put it to the back of his mind, but it did not take much for the memories to come flooding back, for his mind to conjure up once more the image of Raynor's mocking smile as he pointed the handgun at the inspector. Of course, Blizzard knew why the memories were so near the surface and would have been surprised if they weren't. He had experienced an uneasy feeling ever since the gangster had been released from prison six months previously after serving eight years of a twelve-year sentence. Blizzard's state of mind was not helped by constant reassurances from colleagues that, since being freed, Raynor had kept to his old haunts on the city's east side and appeared to have retired from crime, his empire having crumbled during his years inside, his place taken by a new generation of criminals. Blizzard, however, remained to be convinced that their story was over.

To banish the thoughts, he picked up another document from the in-tray and tried to focus on its contents. However, on seeing the words 'multi-agency task force consultation document' in the heading, he sighed and tossed the report back onto the tray: life was too short for such matters, he decided. Anything with the word multi-agency should be directed to the round filing cabinet, that had always been Blizzard's approach to things. He chuckled; that was one of George Moore's favourite sayings as well. But thought of George took his mind back to Harry Josephs and Harry Josephs took him to Morrie Raynor — and the showreel began to play once more.

'For God's sake, man,' murmured the inspector.

There was a light knock on the door and he looked up with relief as a tall, lean man entered the room. Detective Sergeant David Colley was, even at this hour, still smartly turned out, his black hair neatly combed, his round, almost boyish, face still clean-shaven and his dark suit crease-free.

'In late,' said the sergeant, nodding at the in-tray. 'The super been banging on at you about paperwork again?'

'I am sure Arthur would be delighted to think that his words have had some effect, but no. Why are you still in?'

'Tying up some loose ends. That assault on Gray Street.'

'The DI said someone had coughed for it?'

'The brother-in-law. He'd been shagging the victim's mother,' grinned Colley. 'Not exactly a looker, either — too much cellulite for my liking.'

Blizzard winced.

'Trouble is,' continued the sergeant, 'just after we bailed the lad, the vic took a turn for the worse. He's just gone into the General. Blues and twos. You probably heard him being taken in if you were at the hospital.'

'We looking at a possible murder?'

'We'll know better in the morning.'

'Fair enough,' said Blizzard, gesturing to the kettle with his mug. 'Make yourself a brew, it's just boiled. And you can give me a top-up while you're at it.'

'How did your visit to George go?' asked the sergeant, as he reached over for Blizzard's mug and busied himself with the drinks. 'He any better?'

'Hard to tell. Two nights ago he was all right, really perky, cracking jokes, yet tonight he looked awful and hardly even knew I was there.'

Blizzard sighed without realizing he had done it. The sergeant half-turned, spoon in hand, and surveyed his boss for a few seconds. Colley gave a slight smile and returned to his tea-making; he'd give it to the count of three. One, two . . .

'It's always later than you think,' said Blizzard gloomily.

And three, thought Colley. He'd give it another three until the inspector came up with another of his other current favourite sayings. Blizzard had always loved his sayings and since George Moore had become ill, he had been positively prolific.

'Remind me not to get old,' said the inspector. 'Tell firearms they can put a bullet in me when I get decrepit.'

'They wondered if next Wednesday was OK?' said Colley, not turning round. 'Apparently, they've got nothing on in the afternoon.'

'Cheeky basket,' said Blizzard, picking up a clutch of files and hurling them at the sergeant. They scattered across the floor.

Colley grinned and handed the mug of tea over to the inspector before retrieving the documents and replacing them in the in-tray. As he did so, he glanced down and noticed the words 'Force early retirement strategy' on one of the sheets. Blizzard saw the sergeant's expression.

'Don't ask, just don't ask,' grunted the inspector, taking a sip of tea and brightening up. 'Hey, here's something interesting. Does the name Harry Josephs mean anything to you?'

'Should it?'

'He's in the next bed to George.'

32

'And?'

'He's a villain.'

'Even villains get ill,' said Colley. 'We should rejoice at the fact. Remember that party we had when Gary Summerson died? As I recall, the super stumped up for a tab down the Red Lion. Why so interested in this Josephs fellow anyway? He wanted for something?'

'Shouldn't think so. The guy must be approaching eighty. It's just that he mentioned the name Morrie and I remembered that Harry Josephs was one of his inner circle and . . . ' The inspector's voice tailed off lamely as he noticed Colley's look. 'You're going to tell me off, aren't you?'

'Not sure a humble sergeant is allowed to do that to a senior officer, but what I would say is 'have you ever heard of paranoia?''

'Yes, but — '

'Come on, I thought you'd moved on from all that,' said Colley with a slight weariness in his voice, it was not the first time they had had the conversation in recent weeks. 'Morrie Raynor is East's problem.'

'Maybe. Oh, I also looked in on Lorraine Hennessey when I was at the hospital.'

'Ah,' said the sergeant, realization dawning, 'that explains the maudlin mood. What made you do that?'

'Just wanted to show my face. I understand you have done the same recently.'

'Yeah,' nodded Colley. 'Last week.'

'Why?'

'I guess it's because that now I've got a daughter, I thought that I kind of . . . well, you know . . . kind of owed it to her because . . . '

The sergeant did not finish the sentence, did not need to. Blizzard nodded his understanding and both men sat and sipped their drinks in silence. After a few moments, Blizzard gave his sergeant a perplexed look.

'Why can't we crack this, David?' he asked. 'Why can't we track down who sold her the gear?'

'You know Drugs Squad's theory — that it was probably some college kid who did not know what they were doing and stopped when Lorraine became ill.'

'Yeah, well, I've heard enough Drugs Squad theories,' said Blizzard, standing up and draining his mug. 'This has been drifting far too long and it's time someone put a foot up their collective backside. We owe it to Lorraine.'

'I agree, and it'll keep you occupied.'

'What?'

'I said it would keep the Drugs Squad occupied,' replied Colley, regretting the slip.

34

'That's not what it sounded like,' said Blizzard suspiciously. 'I'm not daft. I know what people have been saying.'

When Colley did not respond, the inspector reached for the jacket hanging across the back of his chair then picked up his car keys from the desk.

'Anyway,' he said, irritation banished in a second, 'it can wait until the morning. Pinto?'

'Na, I'll skip that, thanks,' said the sergeant, taking the mugs over to the kettle. 'I told Jay I'd be home at a decent time to look after the babby. It's her first night out and she's going to that new wine bar with some friends.'

'Are you sure they'll let a baby in?'

'They grow up quick these days, guv,' grinned Colley. 'After all, it is, as you are always telling us, later than you think.'

'It certainly is,' said Blizzard, and the two men walked out into the corridor, the inspector snapping out the light and plunging the office into darkness. 'It certainly is.'

* * *

The four grey-haired men sat in the dim back room of The Mitre, a pub in one of the many back streets in Hafton's East End. As the clock on the wall moved on to 11.50, an icy chill entered the room as the door from the street opened. The room fell silent as in walked a slim man with thinning brown hair streaked with grey, and features that were gaunt and sunken. Morrie Raynor was wearing black trousers and a brown jacket, from which he flicked snowflakes before surveying the men. Each of them shifted uncomfortably under his gaze.

'So,' he said in a thin, almost flute-like, voice, 'have I got anything to worry about?'

5

NOVEMBER 1986

Just before 11 p.m., John Blizzard stood up in his office at Abbey Road and prepared to make the short walk to the briefing room, revelling in a moment that he felt ever more strongly would define his career. It was a career that had already enjoyed rapid advancement; only in his early thirties, Blizzard had recently been promoted to detective inspector in charge of Western's Drugs Squad, the youngest in its history. Now, Morrie Raynor had offered him the chance to silence those who doubted his ability to do the job.

Raynor's career had also been a rapid progression; having started off as a small-time villain in the 1960s, he had rapidly become one of the city's most feared gangland figures. Blizzard had never dealt with him during his time on the east side and the event that had set the two men on a collision course now had started when news reached Western Division Drugs Squad that large amounts of heroin had started to appear on the division's streets — and that Morrie Raynor was the source. Having already flooded housing estates on the east side with the drug, Raynor saw the west side as ideal for expansion and Blizzard had taken upon himself the task of halting his ambitions. Officers on the east side had dismissed his chances of success and even the top brass in Western Division were sceptical; no one had ever managed to get charges to stick against Morrie Raynor. Witnesses seemed to melt away whenever the police got close. Walking down the corridor, Blizzard hoped that was all about to change.

He strode into the packed briefing room. There was a feeling of tension in the air and few spoke amid the sombre atmosphere. The officers looked expectantly at the detective inspector as he walked to the front of the room. Some of the older hands regarded him with barely disguised scepticism; they'd seen hotshots come and hotshots go. Blizzard himself, fighting the nerves that came with planning his first major operation, tried to appear relaxed and to ignore the churning sensation in his stomach.

His mood was not helped by the brooding presence of the division's CID chief sitting in the corner of the room. Detective Superintendent Hurley and Blizzard had experienced several differences of opinion since the young

DI had taken up his posting. The superintendent had counselled against the night's operation, arguing that a more considered approach was required. Harsh words had been spoken and voices had been raised, the superintendent arguing that Blizzard lacked the experience to handle such a responsibility, the young detective accusing his superior of being 'old school' and scared to confront a changing world. Eventually, Hurley had given his support — partly because he hoped that failure would bring the brash young DI down a notch or two. Three days since their argument, however, Blizzard's words still rankled with him.

'Do you want to say anything, sir?' asked Blizzard, trying to strike a respectful tone as he looked at the superintendent.

'No, I am sure you are quite capable of handling this yourself.' The superintendent was unable to conceal the iciness in his tone.

Blizzard ignored the comment and started his address, thankful that his voice sounded calm and measured.

'Ladies and gentlemen,' he said, 'let us be under no illusion that if we fail tonight, this division is facing a grave situation. We've seen what heroin has done to the east side and we simply cannot afford to let the same happen on our patch. For me, there can be no argument about it.'

Blizzard glanced at the superintendent, whose face remained impassive, but many of the younger officers nodded their agreement and there were some claps from the gathering; all those in the room had been alarmed at the rapid advance that heroin had made in their division.

'Our main target tonight,' continued Blizzard, pointing to a photograph pinned to the wall, showing a sallow-faced man with thinning brown hair, a piercing stare and a mocking smile, 'is Morris Raynor, better known as Morrie. Aged fifty-one, so he's not exactly a spring chicken.'

Blizzard paused and several of those present gave low laughs. Most didn't — everyone knew that the superintendent was the same age. A couple of officers glanced across at him but his face betrayed no emotion.

'Now,' continued Blizzard, 'I know that many of you will have heard our Eastern colleagues refer to Morrie Raynor as untouchable — you may also have heard such comments entertained in this police station as well — but let me make it absolutely clear that nobody, but nobody, is an untouchable in this division.'

There were murmurs of agreement from

the assembled officers; this was the kind of thing they wanted to hear. They knew how frustrated Eastern officers had been at their inability to bring Morrie Raynor to court and at what they saw as a lack of support from the brass. There had been all sorts of wild rumours, of senior officers being bribed, of secret pacts with police commanders. Blizzard, for his part, believed none of them. The more senior officers among the ranks glanced at each other, impressed by what they were hearing, by the electricity in the room, by the thought that finally they could see their force bring Morrie Raynor to book. They had all heard about the taunts from underworld figures whenever his name was mentioned.

'And now,' continued the inspector, 'Raynor has made a mistake. Tonight, he is bringing in a large shipment of heroin supplied by a gang from the East Midlands. He regards these guys as so important that he has broken his own rule and has agreed to take delivery personally. We believe the drop will take place in an old warehouse down on the West Quay. We will be waiting for him, ladies and gentlemen.'

An hour later the police teams were in place, their vehicles parked up close to a disused fish warehouse which stood on part of the old docklands lining the River Haft's route towards the sea. Once thriving areas, the docklands had mirrored the city's decline during the seventies and eighties, the fishing fleet destroyed, the shipyards falling silent, cranes rusting away, buildings derelict and dilapidated with gaping holes in their walls, gashes torn in their roofs and dust settling on floors once filled with holler and clatter. A keen student of social history away from his police duties, John Blizzard never failed to experience a sadness when he surveyed such places.

The inspector sat in a vehicle parked a hundred metres from the warehouse, peering through the limited light offered by the pale sliver of a moon and eagerly seeking out movement on the wasteland surrounding the building. Next to him in the passenger seat was the superintendent. Neither man had spoken since they had arrived. Alone with his thoughts, Blizzard preferred it that way and he occasionally allowed his gaze to stray to the brown waters of the nearby river. Winding his window down, he could hear the lapping of the waves against the jetties and the distant hum of traffic on the ring road. The noise helped keep him calm.

'You're taking a big risk,' said Hurley eventually. 'I've gone out on a limb letting you do this.'

'Don't think I don't appreciate it.' Blizzard turned to look at the senior officer. 'You've made the right decision, sir.'

'I hope so, because balls this up, sonny Jim, and you can say goodbye to any further promotions while I'm in charge of CID at Abbey Road. I can tell you that for nothing. In fact, if I had my way, you'd already be doing fucking school crossing patrols.'

'Thank you for your support,' murmured Blizzard. 'You don't know what it means.'

But he did.

Shortly after one in the morning, a set of car headlights picked their way through the darkness and both officers heard tyres crunching on the broken glass and old bricks that littered the disused road through the wasteland.

'Stand by,' said Blizzard quietly into the radio.

The car pulled up outside the warehouse and, carried on the still night air, the detectives heard the grating of the giant double doors as they were pulled open, then closed again. Silence returned to the area but they could see a dim light from inside the building. Within minutes, a Transit van could be seen picking its way along the same road, its lights dancing as the vehicle struck the potholes. Again, the officers heard the grating of the doors and the van's lights disappeared from view as the vehicle entered the building.

'We'll give them five minutes,' said Blizzard.

'Your shout,' replied the superintendent, trying to appear unconcerned but, despite himself, feeling a rising tide of excitement at the thought of the forthcoming events.

When the five minutes was up, Blizzard started the engine and the car edged forward. Other vehicles did the same, closing in on the warehouse. Reaching the building first, Blizzard leapt out and started to wrench open the doors, soon joined by several uniformed officers. As the doors swung open, one of the police drivers put his lights on full beam to illuminate a group of panicking men already frantically jumping back into their vehicles.

'Police!' shouted Blizzard, running into the building.

The Transit van gunned its engine and, with a screech of tyres, shot across the ware-house, scattering officers, careering through the doors and ploughing into one of the waiting police cars. The rending of metal and hissing of the ruptured radiator followed by the blaring of the van's horn filled the night air along with shouts as officers dragged out the protesting occupants and wrestled them to the ground.

Still in the warehouse, Morrie Raynor got out of his car and gazed in horror as more police vehicles blocked his escape. He started to run towards the back of the warehouse, followed by one of his henchmen. The henchman swerved to the right as more officers closed on him and threw himself through one of the shattered windows, hitting the ground outside with a squeal as his ankle twisted, but still managing to limp across the wasteland and vanish into the darkness, pursued by officers.

Morrie Raynor was not so fortunate and, on reaching the end of the warehouse and realizing that there was no way out, he whirled round and glared balefully at the approaching Blizzard.

'Who told you?' snarled Raynor. 'Whoever he is, he's a dead man!'

'All words, Morrie. Come on, give it up.'

The inspector's eyes widened as Raynor produced a handgun from his jacket pocket. None of the intelligence they had received had suggested that Raynor or any of his acolytes would be armed. The inspector's voice assumed an alarmed tone.

'Come on, Morrie,' he said, 'don't do anything stupid.'

'Who said it would be stupid? I ain't going to prison. Let me go or I'll put one in you, so help me God.'

'What would that achieve?' said Blizzard,

trying to sound calm. 'Just put down the weapon. There's no way out.'

'There's always a way out,' said Raynor, glancing beyond the inspector to where other officers, including the superintendent, had now halted, watching the confrontation in horror. Raynor gave a mocking smile and pointed the gun at Blizzard.

'I'll shoot him if any of you takes another step forward!' he shouted.

'Let's not be hasty,' said the superintendent. 'I am sure we can work something out.'

'Then let me walk out of here,' said Raynor, still pointing the gun at Blizzard. 'With him for insurance.'

'Well, maybe we can negotiate something around — ' began the superintendent.

'No maybes,' said Blizzard, glancing fiercely back at the senior officer then back at the drug dealer. 'Put the gun down, Morrie. What will you get for drug trafficking — six years? Maybe seven? Murder a copper and they throw away the key. You know that.'

Raynor stared at Blizzard, who tried to stop himself shaking as he looked at the gun barrel. To his relief, he noticed that Raynor's hand was also trembling and that his face betrayed his confusion. After a few moments, Raynor nodded and lowered the gun, letting it drop to the floor with a clatter. Blizzard gave a sigh of relief and, eager to make the arrest, ran forward, snatching up the weapon and handing it to other officers. Two detectives wrestled Raynor to the ground, wrenched his arms behind his back and snapped the handcuffs on his wrists before hauling him to his feet. As they started to lead him past Blizzard, the inspector took a step forward.

'Of course,' said Blizzard, smiling sweetly, 'for pointing a gun at a copper, they'll probably throw away the key anyway. Should have slugged me when you had the chance, Morrie. Should have slugged me.'

Raynor gave the detective a mocking smile.

'One day,' he said quietly, 'I will.'

★ ★ ★

'You coming to bed, love?' said Fee, walking into the living room to where Blizzard was sitting in an armchair, a half-finished pint of beer in hand, having long gone flat.

Blizzard started, dragged from his reverie by the comment. For a moment, he looked round the room, almost as if he was not sure where he was. Then he glanced at her pyjamas.

'Is that the time?' he said, glancing at the clock and noticing to his surprise that it read 11.30.

'Did you fall asleep?' she said, coming to stand behind the chair, leaning over and putting her arms round him. 'Perhaps you really are getting old. Maybe a nice cup of Horlicks will help.'

'Thank you for those few kind words,' grunted the inspector. 'Colley was similarly complimentary about my advancing years earlier today. Seems that every bastard has decided that I'm ready to pick up my pension.'

Almost without realizing it, Blizzard sighed. Fee walked round to the front of the chair and crouched down before the inspector.

'What's wrong?' she asked.

'Nothing.'

'It doesn't look like nothing, pet.' She frowned. 'You weren't thinking about this stupid Harry Josephs stuff, were you?'

' 'Course not.' He noticed her expression, a mixture of scepticism and concern. 'Well, a bit, maybe.'

'But we've been through this before, love.' Her voice was soft now and she rubbed his hand as she spoke. 'It's all a game, you know that. That's why Morrie Raynor said what he said that night. Besides, you've been threatened like that a thousand times before.'

'I know,' said Blizzard quietly, 'but all the other times I never believed that they meant it.'

Shortly before 1.30, an inebriated Geoff Bates finally emerged from the warmth of the back-street east-side public house into the sharp chill of a winter's night. He had remained in The Mitre long after Morrie Raynor had departed, consuming more pints than he could count. Now, Geoff Bates was drunk. Cursing as he struggled to fasten his coat, he gave up and stepped unsteadily onto a pavement already glistening with gathering frost. That was when he noticed for the first time the lone figure standing at the end of the street. Bates felt a tug of fear as the stranger started to walk slowly towards him, the pace steady and unhurried. Peering closer, Bates recognized the features and tensed.

'What you doing here?' he asked nervously.

His voice tailed off as the figure raised a hand and Bates saw that it contained a handgun.

'Hey, what you doing?' cried Bates in alarm. 'Come on, put the gun down.'

'Sorry, Geoff. I can't take the risk. Not now. You know he won't survive prison.'

The shot dropped Geoff Bates where he stood.

6

The next afternoon found a dramatic change in George Moore's demeanour and when Blizzard walked into the ward, his friend sat up in bed and gestured frantically with his hand. Troubled by the previous night's experience, Blizzard had broken his usual custom of evening visits and slipped out of Abbey Road shortly before two to make the short drive to the General Hospital in time for visiting hours. He knew that it was not concern for George that had drawn him back to the place so soon, that he really wanted to take another look at Harry Josephs.

As the inspector was walking up the hospital stairs, however, he had begun to doubt the wisdom of the move, struggling to justify to himself his overwhelming desire to see Josephs again. As he made his usual stop at the top of the stairs to mop sweat from his brow and carry out his customary cursory tidying-up exercise, he almost turned back, but when one of the nurses from the ward passed him by and gave him a bright smile, he realized that he had to go through with it. Couldn't risk George thinking that he had ducked out on him.

His friend's behaviour when Blizzard walked into the ward temporarily drove any thought of Harry Josephs from the inspector's mind. Walking across to George's bed, the inspector realized that he had not seen him so animated for a long time, the old man's eyes bright, the expression on his face the look of someone desperate to impart information. George indicated that he wanted the inspector to lean over. He had a conspiratorial look about him.

'You all right, George?' asked Blizzard. 'You look a bit — '

'Take me out into the lounge,' whispered George.

'What?'

'The lounge, man. Get a wheelchair and take me there, I have something to tell you.' Moore glanced at Harry Josephs, who appeared to be asleep, mouthing silent words. 'Something I do not want him to hear.'

'I'll check with a nurse if — '

'Just do it,' hissed George, grabbing hold of the inspector's coat sleeve.

Blizzard shrugged and went to find a nurse, this time allowing himself a longer look at Harry Josephs as he passed. The old man had just sat up in the bed, his lips still moving silently as he talked to himself. Blizzard could not hear what he was saying. Out in the corridor, the inspector saw a grey-haired woman heading for the nurses' station.

'George wants to go into the lounge,' he said. 'Would that be OK, Sister?'

'Might calm him down,' said Maureen Cox. 'He's been like a cat on a hot tin roof today. It's not good for him in his condition.'

'Is it his illness making him like this?'

'They can go through phases, especially if there's a bit of dementia kicking in, but I get the impression that there's something else troubling your friend.'

'Like what?' asked Blizzard.

'I was rather hoping that you would tell me, Inspector. He's been waiting for you to arrive. Keeps demanding to know the time and looking towards the door. Getting this agitated is really not good for him, you know. He needs to be as calm as possible. Take that wheelchair over there if you need it.'

Blizzard walked back into the side room, pushing the chair. Josephs had his eyes open now and when he saw the inspector, he pointed a bony finger at him.

'Is that you, Geoff?' he said.

Blizzard shook his head.

'Sorry,' he said. 'Again.'

'Well, if you see him tell him to be careful.' Josephs leaned forwards and lowered his voice. 'You know what Morrie is like. He'll have you as soon as look at you.'

Blizzard stared at him, but did not have chance to reply because George Moore gestured frantically for the inspector to bring the wheelchair over.

'See what I mean?' said the old man urgently. 'We got to get this sorted, John, I'm telling you. We got to get this sorted.'

Two minutes later, the old man having donned his dressing-gown with some difficulty then slumped heavily into the wheelchair, they entered the large and deserted lounge at the end of the ward.

'No one in?' asked George anxiously.

'No.'

'Good. We don't want anyone hearing.'

'Hearing what, George?' said Blizzard. 'You really are not making any sen — '

'Park me by the window and shut the door.'

Blizzard wheeled the chair over to the picture window and went back to close the door. Returning to George, the inspector looked out at the expanse of Hafton city centre stretched before them, the roofs glistening with ice; the temperature had not lifted above freezing all day, despite the wan sun struggling to be seen through the tatters of clouds. As ever, he was struck by the sight.

'Quite a view — ' began Blizzard.

'Forget the bloody view,' said George. 'You heard him as well, didn't you?'

'Heard who, George?'

'Come on, John, don't play the fool with me,' said George, as the inspector dragged a chair across and sat down. 'Don't try to tell me you didn't recognize him.'

'All I saw,' said Blizzard, mindful of the sister's warning about agitating him any further, 'was a seriously ill old man who — '

'I knew who he was the moment I saw him, of course.'

'Try to keep calm,' said Blizzard, noticing with alarm the wild look in his friend's eyes. 'The sister said that you had been getting yourself worked up about something.'

'Too right I am,' nodded George vigorously. 'Harry Josephs was one of Morrie Raynor's gang, surely you know that?'

For a few moments more, Blizzard fought the battle, torn between the sister's entreaty and a growing intrigue at the words that Harry Josephs had been uttering. The detective's instinct won out — it usually did.

'OK, George,' nodded Blizzard. 'Yes, I know who he is.'

'Finally,' said George, sitting back in the wheelchair with a look of satisfaction. 'So are you going to investigate?'

'Investigate what?' Blizzard was genuinely surprised by the question.

George lowered his voice and glanced round the room before continuing.

'They called Harry the Secrets Man,' he said. 'The one in whom Raynor confided. Well, he's in with an infection and he's been talking non-stop. You've seen what he's like.'

'Yeah, and I've seen what you're like,' said Blizzard, trying to retain his sense of perspective.

'OK, I admit that most of what Harry Josephs is saying is rubbish but occasionally he says something that makes sense. This morning, he mentioned Des Fairley.'

'Yeah, he mentioned a guy called Des last night.'

'Well, you know who he was?'

'Not really.'

'Before your time I guess,' said George. 'Des Fairley was an unsolved murder from the sixties. Killed outside The Kestrel over on the east side back in 1967. Surely you remember me talking about it when we were at Eastern together.'

'Jesus, was that him, was it? Shot?'

'That's the one. Dropped as he came out of the boozer. Very professional.'

'You reckon it was a hit?'

'No doubt about it. Des Fairley wasn't any

old villain. At the time he died, he was Morrie Raynor's right-hand man, but the night it happened, he had been shooting his mouth off in the pub, acting like he wasn't scared of Morrie.'

'Never a good idea.'

'Exactly. People tried to shut him up, then . . . ' George made the shape of a gun with his right hand. 'Only unsolved murder case I ever worked on.'

'Are you sure Harry Josephs is talking about the same guy, though? I mean, he's not exactly in the best state of mind, is he? And are you sure you're not mistaken, for that matter? Sorry, George, don't take this the wrong way but a fortnight ago you thought that I was a vicar. Been called many things but — '

'Don't patronize me,' said George, glaring at him. 'Harry Josephs was tied up with the murder of Des Fairley, I am sure of it. Him and Geoff Bates.'

'One of them the shooter, you think?'

'No. We always reckoned that Raynor brought in a hitman but I always wondered if Josephs or Bates made the call to him that night.'

'I thought you said they tried to stop Fairley getting himself in trouble?'

'Yeah, but think about it, John,' said

George, his eyes shining as he rolled back the years. 'When he refused to shut up, I reckon they thought that with him out of the way, they would both be moved up in the pecking order.'

'Bates was certainly a player by the time Raynor tried to move into Western,' nodded Blizzard. 'I always reckoned he was the one who escaped when we raided the warehouse down West Quay. Just couldn't prove it. Didn't know that much about Josephs, mind.'

'That's because Harry stayed over on the east side. He never really agreed with Raynor's decision to move into drugs. Old school was Harry Josephs.'

'Well, it's all very interesting,' said Blizzard, walking over to stare out of the window, noting without much surprise that it had started to snow again, 'but not sure that it means much. Des Fairley was killed thirty years ago and Harry Josephs is a sick old man.'

'Maybe he is, but like I said, he always kept his mouth shut. Until now. Now he's saying all sorts of things that should interest you.'

'Things?' said Blizzard, turning back into the room. 'What things?'

'Just fragments. They would not make any sense to most people but they do to me. Jobs we never solved. I am pretty sure that this afternoon he was talking about a security van job over on the east side in seventy-seven. And I am damned sure he mentioned a bank job on Moss Street. Same year as I recall. A bank clerk got coshed on that one. Fractured skull. We always reckoned that Morrie Raynor organized them to fund the setting up of his drugs network.'

'All very interesting, George,' said Blizzard, 'but it's history now. And ancient history at that.'

★ ★ ★

Alex Mather was drinking in a pub on one of the city's east-side housing estates when his mobile rang. He glanced down at the number as the call cut out after three rings. Always three rings. Mather casually finished his pint and walked out into the street where he ducked down an alleyway. Satisfied that no one had followed him, he returned the call.

'What you got?' he asked, recognizing his informant's voice.

'You know I said I might have something interesting on that kid who took the drugs?'

'Yeah.'

'Usual place — an hour.'

'Don't be late,' said Mather.

The line went dead.

★ ★ ★

'Maybe it's not ancient history,' said George Moore as the inspector sat down again. 'Last night, three dodgy characters turned up to see Harry. I was asleep so did not see what happened, but I heard this morning that there was an argument with the nurses.'

'What about?'

'If you ask me, they were after getting heavy with Harry. They're scared about what he might say,' and George's eyes gleamed. 'What if Harry is starting to reveal his secrets? Forget TLC, my boy, this is more like TIC.'

He grinned at his joke.

'Sorry, not sure I can see it,' said Blizzard, making one last attempt to retain perspective.

'Think about it, John. The last thing Raynor wants is to go back to prison — everyone knows he had a rough time of it in there. And now what happens? Suddenly there's a loose cannon.'

'OK, say you're right,' said the inspector, 'what are you suggesting I do?'

'We have to act fast. Sometimes these infections only last a day or two. We need to start monitoring what Josephs says. Maybe bring someone in undercover.' He gave Blizzard another toothy grin. 'I always thought that young lady of yours would look nice in a nurse's uniform. I'd get better if she was bed-bathing me.'

Blizzard gave him a pained look.

'Come on,' said George, serious again. 'You always said that it was a disgrace when Raynor got out after only eight years. Don't tell me you don't fancy another crack at him?'

'Has Josephs recognized you?'

'Don't think so. He called me Beryl this morning.'

'You do realize that even if we do get anything, just about all of it will relate to the Eastern and I would be duty bound to hand it over to their CID?'

'Your governor will swing things. Arthur Ronald still has plenty of friends in Eastern.' George closed his eyes and sat back in the wheelchair.

'You OK?' asked Blizzard.

'I feel a bit tired.' The voice was suddenly weak. 'Take me back now, will you?'

Having seen George back into bed, unsurprised when he did not respond to the inspector's farewell, a pensive Blizzard was walking down the corridor when Sister Cox approached him.

'Did he say what was troubling him?' she asked.

'Memories,' said Blizzard. 'Just memories.'

60

'Ah, but whose memories?' said the sister, and walked back down the corridor. 'Now there is the question.'

The comment stayed with the inspector as he drove back to the police station.

★ ★ ★

The late afternoon temperature had already dipped below freezing when the lone figure made its way through the freezing fog starting once more to shroud the city. Standing in the shadows at the far side of the hospital car-park was Malky, a young man with a cap tipped over his face to conceal his features. He shrank further back into the darkness as the new arrival approached and handed him a plastic carrier bag.

'You sure no one suspects?' asked Malky, peering into the bag.

'Relax.' The voice was confident. 'The police don't even know we've started up again. You in or not?'

'Yeah, I'm in,' said Malky.

'You going to do the same as last time?' asked the man.

'Yeah.'

'Then get the fucking mix right. We don't want another Lorraine Hennessey.'

'Trust me.'

61

'I trusted you last time. It's not just me this time, sunshine.'

'What do you mean by that?'

The man did not reply, turned and walked back towards the hospital.

7

Blizzard was still thinking about the sister's comment as he walked through the corridors of Abbey Road Police Station half an hour after leaving the hospital. He could not help feel that he had somehow allowed himself to be bounced into agreeing with George's plan. Was his friend imagining everything, he asked himself? Were past and present getting mixed up in his mind? Was Blizzard making a mistake in even listening to his friend's conspiracy theories in the first place? Away from the cocooned surroundings of the hospital, and from George Moore's fierce determination, the inspector had to admit that it all sounded less obvious. He found himself questioning the wisdom of the promises that he had made. He arrived at the CID room at Abbey Road to see Colley sitting at his desk. The sergeant looked up from the document he was reading.

'Anything exciting?' asked Blizzard.

'The forensics report on Gray Street. Ross reckons that we have enough to make a case stick. Fibres on his pullover.'

'How's the vic doing?'

'Missing his mother.' Colley gave a sly look. 'Or anyone's mother really.'

Blizzard raised his eyes to the ceiling.

'Sorry,' grinned Colley. 'Hospital reckons he'll pull through. Talked to Ramsey and he said stick with ABH. Anyway, where you been? I came along to your office three times and you weren't there. No one seemed to know where you had gone.'

'What was important that it couldn't wait?' Blizzard wandered over to stare out of the window at the gathering mid-afternoon gloom.

'Nothing really. So where *were* you?'

'If you must know,' said Blizzard, turning round, 'I went to see George Moore.'

'Thought you went in the evenings. He taken a turn for the worse?'

'The opposite really. Haven't seen him that well for weeks.' Blizzard hesitated. 'Look, I know this might sound a bit left field, David, but he reckons he's onto something interesting about Morrie Raynor.'

'Ah.' The sergeant's tone was flat. 'That again.'

'Yeah. See, George reckons that some of Raynor's heavies might be out to stop Josephs spilling the beans.' Blizzard was warming to his theme now. 'Now, let's just assume for a moment that Harry Josephs is in some kind of danger and . . . '

Blizzard paused as another officer walked into the squad room. Aged in his mid-thirties, Chris Ramsey was one of the division's two detective inspectors: the organizer, the one who drew up the rosters and allocated the manpower. A slim, tall man with short-cropped brown hair, he had an angular face, a prominent nose and a thin mouth not particularly given to laughing. Blizzard eyed him for a moment, hesitating to elaborate on his comments because although Ramsey was a conscientious detective, he was also an unspectacular man little given to inventive thinking, in the DCI's view. Blizzard doubted if the detective inspector would appreciate what he had been about to say. Best to say nothing, he decided. Without realizing he had even done it, Blizzard gave a little nod. Yes, best to say nothing in the circumstances.

'The guv'nor's been to see George Moore,' explained Colley, looking at Ramsey. 'Reckons the old man's onto something interesting.'

Blizzard glared at Colley but said nothing.

'Not about the deranged Harry Josephs, by any chance?' said Ramsey, unable to conceal the scepticism from his voice as he took a seat at one of the desks, crossed his arms and eyed the DCI without much enthusiasm. 'Because if you're about to ask me to release officers for some kind of wild goose chase just because — '

Ramsey did not complete the sentence. He did not need to. Blizzard had already realized that George Moore's theories were starting to sound ever more lame and the dubious reaction of Ramsey and Colley was hardly improving the situation. Under their sceptical gaze, Blizzard's usual confidence started to ebb away. Noticing that the others were looking at him expectantly, he tried to look nonchalant.

'Look, I'm not saying George is right, all I'm saying is that he reckons someone might be out to silence Harry Josephs.'

'But Josephs must be at least eighty,' protested Ramsey. 'As is George — and not exactly in the best state of mind, from what Dave tells me.'

Blizzard glowered at Colley again but said nothing.

'Besides,' continued Ramsey, 'even if Morrie Raynor is back in business, the last thing Ronald will want is you interfering in Eastern's affairs. He's got enough trouble with you interfering in affairs over here.'

'What does that mean?' said Blizzard sharply.

'Everyone knows you'll do anything to avoid finishing those reports.' Irritation crept into Ramsey's tone. 'I even heard one of the secretaries say you were asking how many paperclips we order. And you've been questioning my rosters, haven't you? I mean, what's wrong with my rosters and whenever did you care anyway?'

'I am not sure what this has got to do with Harry Josephs,' said Blizzard, chewing his lip.

'All I am saying is are you sure you're not getting excited about this because it's something to do?' said Ramsey. 'You've never coped well when things are quiet. You get bored too easily. Look, I don't want to question your judgement, guv — '

'But I imagine you're going to,' said Blizzard sourly.

Ramsey eyed the inspector uneasily and there was a heavy silence in the room for a few moments. Colley, not wishing to be part of the discussion and regretting making his initial comment, looked out of the window, noting that it had started to snow again.

'Go on, Chris,' said Blizzard. 'Say what's on your mind.'

'Look, everyone knows it's personal between you and Morrie Raynor.' Ramsey's tone was more respectful now. 'I know that George Moore is a friend and ex-job and all that . . . '

'I understand what you're saying, but he *was* talking about an unsolved murder over on the east side back in 1967. I can't ignore that.'

'Yes, but it's old news, guv. Raynor and his cronies are living in the past. I'm sorry, but I am much more interested in today. I've just been compiling the crime stats for the past twenty-four hours. Our quiet period has well and truly come to an end. Eight burglaries on the Lakeside alone, a couple of shop robberies over on the Marchbank and Dave's assault on Gray Street.' The DI gestured to a pile of folders on one of the desks. 'So if you're looking for something to do — '

Ramsey was interrupted by the ringing of Blizzard's mobile phone and, relieved at the distraction, the chief inspector took the call.

'Blizzard,' he said.

'It's Mather.'

'Bloody Hell,' exclaimed Blizzard, walking out into the corridor and lowering his voice. 'Thought you were dead.'

'Not quite. Got a question for you. Lorraine Hennessey. Anything happening with the case?'

'Lot of dead ends. Why?'

'Just had an informant of mine on — says he knows something.'

'Any idea what?'

'Not yet.'

'You meeting him again?'

'Yeah. Soon.'

'Let me know, will you?' said Blizzard.

'Sure.' There was a moment's hesitation at the other end. 'John?'

'Yeah, I'm still here, Alex.'

'Just be careful, yeah?'

The call went dead and Blizzard walked thoughtfully back into the squad room.

'Anything?' asked Ramsey.

'Not sure yet. Getting back to what we were talking about, all I am saying is that it might be worth keeping an eye on Harry Josephs, maybe trying to find out what his old mucker is up to. Chap called Geoff Bates. What are you looking at me like that for, Chris?'

'Because I have this awful feeling that I know exactly what he's up to. I've just come off the phone from one of the Eastern inspectors. That guy who was shot last night? The one whose face was so badly mangled that they were struggling to ID him? Well, they've just got a name.'

'And do I take it,' said Blizzard quietly, 'that someone has murdered Geoff Bates?'

Ramsey nodded.

'Maybe,' said Colley, 'old George Moore's Almanac is not as wacko as some of us might think.'

'A prophet in his own land, lads,' beamed

Blizzard, walking towards the squad room door. 'A prophet in his own land.'

They listened until the sound of his footsteps faded into the distance.

'You do know, I take it,' said Ramsey eventually, 'that he'll be insufferable now?'

'Now?' grinned the sergeant. 'What's so special about now?'

8

Shortly before 6.30 p.m., with the winter light having long since faded to be replaced by blackness, seventeen-year-old Bobby Leyton waited nervously in the back alley that ran behind the rundown row of shops on the Radcliffe Estate. As he waited, the student stamped his feet and rubbed his hands together to combat the cold. At one point, a shop worker emerged from one of the back yards, the grating of the wooden gate causing the teenager to start.

'What you doing there?' asked the shop worker suspiciously, as he placed a black sack of rubbish out in the alleyway. 'Sod off, or I'll call the police.'

'I ain't up to no trouble,' protested Leyton, turning the peak of his cap down further so that his features were masked from view. 'I'm just waiting.'

'Waiting? What for?'

'Just waiting.'

'Yeah, well, if it's for a bus it'll be a long wait then, the number five don't stop here no more,' said the man and disappeared back into the yard, chuckling at his joke. The gate grated shut.

The teenager scowled and turned to look towards the end of the alley, tensing as a figure appeared round the corner. Unable to see the man's identify in the gathering gloom, he only relaxed when the new arrival was a few feet away and he was able to recognize features which had been partially concealed by the hood.

'You been here long?' asked the visitor.

'Long enough, Malky,' said Leyton. 'Freezing my nuts off. You got it?'

'Yeah,' said Malky, producing a small package from his jacket pocket.

'It safe this time?'

'Safe enough,' said Malky. 'Do you want the stuff or not?'

'How much?'

'Thirty-five.'

'Hang on, last time it was only twenty.'

'It's supply and demand, ain't it?' Malky gave a dry laugh. 'One of your subjects is economics — you should understand about market forces. Blame Adam Smith.'

Bobby Leyton scowled again and handed over a roll of notes. Malky shoved them into his jeans pocket, turned without a word and disappeared into the darkness.

★ ★ ★

72

'For God's sake, John, don't you have enough to keep you busy over here?' asked Arthur Ronald, the exasperation clear in his voice as the two men sat in the detective superintendent's Abbey Road office. 'By my reckoning there's at least three reports that you haven't even bothered to do. I thought we agreed that, since it was quiet, you would get them finished.'

'Yeah, sorry about that, Arthur. Got sidetracked on other things, I am afraid. You know how it is.'

'Unfortunately, I do,' sighed Ronald, looking across the desk at his DCI. 'Although quite why you are suddenly showing an interest in our supply of paperclips is beyond me.'

'Ah, you heard about that, did you?'

'Heard about it? The whole police station is talking about it. And Ramsey hasn't shut up about his blessed rosters either. I mean, what's wrong with his rosters?' Blizzard opened his mouth to reply but closed it as the superintendent continued, 'And as for being sidetracked, surely this George Moore thing is the perfect example. The man always did have an over-active imagination.'

'Yes, but Geoff Bates being murdered isn't imaginary, is it?' said the inspector. 'I thought you'd be delighted that he's dead.'

'I'm absolutely overjoyed at his untimely demise — 'bout time someone blew his head off — but it's an Eastern case. You know that.'

'Ah, yes, but Harry Josephs is in a hospital in our patch and George reckons you can pull a few strings with Eastern to get us in on it.'

'So now we're taking instructions from George Moore, are we?' said Ronald sourly. 'Even if I did believe his cock-and-bull story, do you realize how complicated it is when you investigate cases out of division?'

'Yes, but — '

'And Eastern are the worst of the lot. You needn't look like that, John. Woe betide the Eastern officer who dares to put a foot into your patch.'

'Yeah, I appreciate that but — '

'You certainly don't make life easy for me.' Ronald sighed again and looked at his friend, his irritation spent as rapidly as it had blown up. 'So, come on then, convince me that there is really something in this.'

Blizzard gave him an affectionate look: Arthur always came round in the end. The men had known each other for more than twenty years, having first worked together as rookie officers before their careers took different paths. Blizzard remained a detective, but Ronald, always the more ambitious for high rank, went back into uniform and served his time around the force before earning the move he craved, command of CID in the constabulary's southern half.

One of Ronald's first decisions was to demand that Blizzard be moved from Western's drugs squad and promoted to detective chief inspector in charge of CID for the division, the largest in the force's southern area and responsible for a significant proportion of its crime. Wary of Blizzard's maverick tendencies, the chief constable had not greeted the request with much enthusiasm. Ronald, however, had had good reason for his obstinance. With crime spiralling in Western Division, he viewed Blizzard as the man to start bringing it down. Ronald was to be proved right; since Blizzard had taken up his new post, detection rates had increased twenty-four per cent and crime was down by almost a third, figures unprecedented in the force. Some said that they were the statistics that kept John Blizzard in a job.

Friends they might be, but they were very different men. University-educated and married with two teenaged children, Ronald was a slightly pudgy, balding man with ruddy cheeks and eyes with bags which sagged darkly. Given to constant worrying about mortgages and university fees, and a little prone, in Blizzard's view, to taking too much notice about what other people thought about him, he was not yet fifty but looked older. A smart dresser with shoes that always shone, a sharply pressed suit and a tie constantly done up, he was a charming man with an easy manner. However, behind the avuncular appearance lurked a hard-headed detective. It was where he and Blizzard had long connected — and where they connected now.

'Go on then,' repeated Ronald. 'Convince me.'

'Well for a start, I'm not stupid, I can see why everyone else is so sceptical about this.'

'George is hardly a reliable witness, is he? He wasn't when he was on the job half the time so God knows what he's like now.'

'He is ill, I grant you,' nodded Blizzard, 'but it's a hell of a coincidence that the day he starts talking about Geoff Bates, the guy gets gunned down in a similar manner to Fairley, which, might I remind you, remains unsolved. All I am saying is that it might be worth us taking a closer look.'

Ronald gave him a sharp look.

'Not planning to arrest Harry Josephs in his hospital bed, I hope? That's all I need after last time.'

'Somehow I don't think that would be a particularly good idea,' said Blizzard, chuckling at the memory of the hospital administrator's fury when he had tried to arrest a bank robber on his way into surgery for appendicitis.

'No need to look so pleased with yourself,' said Ronald tartly.

'Sorry.' Blizzard tried to look serious. 'No, all I am asking is if I can have a word with someone over on Eastern, purely on the QT, nothing official. Max Randall, maybe. See what their thinking is.'

'OK, talk to him, but I do not want you wasting too much time on this. And I don't want you poking about the General Hospital either.'

'I did apologize to the administrator over the arrest thing.'

'I've seen your apologies,' said Ronald bleakly. 'Besides, I think he's more concerned about your performance at his Christmas do. I knew it was a mistake to invite you. I don't think he appreciated being asked if his pharmacy might have supplied the drugs that damn near killed Lorraine Hennessey.'

'I'm glad you've mentioned her, Arthur. Even before Mather rang me, I was beginning to think that it might be worth taking another look at the case.'

'Mather rang you?' Ronald looked surprised. 'I thought he was dead.'

'He reckons one of his informants has got something on the Hennessey case.' Blizzard hesitated, loath to further irritate the superintendent. 'Look, Arthur, I know you have given Heather Morrison your backing on this one, but I really would like to take a more active role in the inquiry.'

'I agree.'

'You do?'

'Yes.' Ronald lowered his voice. 'Between you and me, John, I'm not sure she's up to the job. I'm hearing a few comments.'

'Does that mean I can take it over?'

'Yeah, that's fine.' Ronald watched Blizzard stand up. 'Before you go. Those reports?'

'On your desk tomorrow, Arthur.' Blizzard turned at the door and nodded gravely. 'Scout's honour.'

'And were you ever a Scout?'

'No.'

Ronald watched his friend walk out into the corridor, sighed and reached into his desk draw to produce a small bottle of aspirin; he could feel one of his headaches coming on.

* * *

Alex Mather stood in the late afternoon darkness and waited for his informant. Feeling the cold wheedling its way into his bones, he glanced at his watch.

'He's late again,' he said with a scowl.

78

The sound of a footstep on the nearby path alerted him and he looked up to see the man approaching.

'Maybe I should buy you a watch,' said the detective. 'What you got for me?'

'That Lorraine Hennessey kid,' said the informant, glancing around to make sure that no one was watching them. 'Whoever pushed the drugs is back at it. Over on the west side again.'

'Same as last time?'

'Yeah.' The informant lowered his voice. 'Except as well as crushing the Valium tablets into the methadone again, they're diluting it to make it go further.'

'Jesus, didn't they learn anything from what happened to Lorraine?' said Mather with a shake of the head. 'What are they diluting it with?'

'Folks reckon it might be vodka.'

'Any idea who's dealing?'

'Already putting my neck on the line telling you this.'

'What, you frightened of some college kid?'

'It's more complicated than that.'

'There's something you're not telling me.' Mather noticed that his informant was sweating despite the chill of the night. 'Why did you ask about Blizzard?'

'No reason.'

'There must be. You wouldn't have asked otherwise.'

'You ain't getting nothing else out of me.' The man looked scared. 'I'm only telling you this because I don't want to see no more kids getting hurt. Could be my little girl one day. You got kids?'

Mather hesitated.

'Yeah,' he said. 'One.'

'You don't sound sure.'

'It's a long story.'

'How old's she?'

'Two.' Mather tried not to show his emotion. 'It was her birthday last week.'

'Well, you look after her. We got to make sure our kids are safe. That's more important than owt else.'

'A most commendable viewpoint. Do I assume it means you won't want paying for this bit of information then?'

The man looked worried and Mather chuckled, reached into his pocket and produced a wad of banknotes, peeling off several and handing them to the informant. Trying not to think about the child he had not seen for the best part of a year, Alex Mather watched in silence as the man scuttled off into the shadows once more. When he was sure that he had gone, the detective produced his mobile phone. Its screen shone bright in the darkness as he dialled the number and he held it underneath his leather jacket to shield the light from view before holding it up to his ear.

'Blizzard,' said a voice.

'Mather again,' said the detective.

'Fuck me, twice in one day, I am honoured.'

'You might not be when I tell you what I've just heard. Sorry, matey, but I am afraid you might have a problem.'

★   ★   ★

Flecks of snow were swirling in the air when the two teenage boys crunched their way across the icy building site a couple of miles to the west of Abbey Road Police Station. The cans of cheap lager rustled in their carrier bags as they made their way towards a far corner of the site, picking their way round builders' equipment in the darkness. After glancing nervously round at the nearby street lights, the boys disappeared behind some trees, close to where the foundations of a new house had been laid out. They had chosen the place to drink their lager with great care, the convergence of two red-brick walls creating a sheltered space concealed from the view of anyone walking down the nearby main road.

'Jesus, it's dark,' said one of the boys, reaching into the bag, producing a can and snapping open the ring pull. 'Can hardly see my hand in front of my face.'

'Got a torch,' said the other boy, reaching into his coat pocket. He chuckled. 'Knew my time in the Scouts would come in handy one day. I'm prepared, see.'

He flashed the light around the den. The beam came to rest on the lifeless face of Bobby Leyton.

9

Shortly after 10.30 next morning, John Blizzard stood and stared silently down at the body of the young man on the table. He thought of Mather's warning the night before, of the way the Lorraine Hennessey inquiry had drifted, of the way she had lain silently in that hospital bed since the day she had drunk the adulterated methadone. Blizzard glanced round at Colley, who was in his customary position leaning against the mortuary wall; he had a troubled expression on his face. The inspector knew that, as the father of a young child, his sergeant would be finding this difficult. Ever since Jay had given birth to their baby daughter, anything to do with young people had triggered a strong response in the detective. Blizzard knew how he felt: as Laura's godparent he had been experiencing similar emotions in the months since the birth.

Not that the inspector had been immune to such sensations before, or so he had always told himself, it was just that he had previously found it easier to regard a young person's body as the same as any other. Part of the job.

A case. A number on a file. However, things had been changing and changing quicker than he liked. After Laura's birth, Fee had started to mention the idea of she and Blizzard also starting a family before, as she had phrased it over a glass of red wine one night, the inspector became 'too old and decrepit to perform'. Given that such thoughts had been occupying more and more of Blizzard's time in recent months, the sight of the young man on the slab in the General Hospital's mortuary was an unwelcome intrusion.

If Blizzard was not surprised at his own reaction to the death, what did surprise him was that the pathologist seemed to be experiencing similar difficulties as they stood around the table. Everyone knew that Blizzard detested Peter Reynolds but this time the normal bad-tempered exchanges between the two men were absent, replaced by a more sombre atmosphere devoid of edge. Both men seemed consumed in the moment, as if overwhelmed by the enormity of a young person's senseless death.

A balding middle-aged little man with piggy eyes gleaming out of a chubby face, and dressed as ever in a shabby, ill-fitting black suit, Reynolds usually gave the impression that he liked being around death, almost revelled in it. This time was different. Whereas he would usually be busying himself around the body, sometimes humming to himself or making poor-taste comments designed to irritate the chief inspector as he poked and prodded the cadaver, this time he also stared down at the young man in silence.

'It's quite a remarkable thing given how long I have been doing the job,' he said quietly, 'but this has never happened to me before.'

'What hasn't?' asked Blizzard.

'Knowing the dead person.'

'Ah,' said Blizzard, not quite sure what to say; he had never even considered the possibility that Peter Reynolds might have feelings. He glanced at Colley, whose face displayed similar bemusement. 'How come you know him?'

'Bobby goes — went — to college with my son. Queen Mary's. He's been round to the house a few times. Wanted to be an artist.' Reynolds gave an approving nod. 'Very talented.'

'What was he like?'

'Nice young man,' said Reynolds. 'I think you could have perhaps described him as somewhat naïve, however. A bit too easily led, if you ask me.'

'Clearly,' said Blizzard, looking at the body.

85

'Such a waste,' said Reynolds sadly. 'He had so much to look forward to.'

Both detectives stared at the pathologist; apart from his constant comments about golf, this was one of the few times in all the post-mortems they had attended with him that they could recall him having ever revealed anything of himself. Neither officer even knew that he had a son. Not that they had ever thought to ask. Looking at the pathologist's expression, Blizzard felt an urge to say that he wished Reynolds would show the same respect for all the other bodies that landed on his table, that you didn't have to know someone to feel a sense of human tragedy, that every victim deserved respect, however young, however old. Somehow it did not seem the right time.

'He was only seventeen, same as my son,' continued Reynolds, peering closer at the body then looking at the inspector. 'One hates to suggest it, Blizzard, but it does look remarkably similar to that Hennessey girl.'

'Lorraine,' said Blizzard. 'Her name's Lorraine.'

Reynolds ignored the comment.

'You said you found a bottle at the scene?' he said.

'We think whoever is doing this has been decanting it into pop bottles,' nodded

Blizzard. 'Our forensics lads reckon it contained methadone, probably mixed with Valium and vodka if what we hear is right.'

'Similar to last time,' nodded Reynolds, 'although the vodka is a new touch. Of course, I cannot be absolutely certain until I carry out the full examination.'

'Do you really want to do it, given that you know the lad?' asked Colley, walking up to the table but not looking down at the body. 'I know I couldn't go through with it.'

'I'll be fine.' Reynolds gave them a slight smile. 'They're all just empty vessels when they're dead, aren't they, Sergeant? Assuming the findings support my initial theory, it sounds like you've got a problem, gentlemen.'

'You're the second person who has told me that,' grunted Blizzard.

'Maybe not, though,' said Colley, finally steeling himself to look down at the boy. He tried to sound hopeful, as if he was attempting to convince himself. 'Lorraine was the only one last time, remember? Maybe she just reacted more seriously than anyone else to what she had taken. Perhaps we will get away with it.'

'Your optimistic approach is commendable, Sergeant,' said Reynolds. He gave the inspector a sly look. 'See, Blizzard, the innocence of youth. We could all learn from it.'

Colley tried not to smile, the sombre atmosphere temporarily banished by the comment. This was more like it. The re-emergence of the old Reynolds was important because the sergeant always found himself besieged by Abbey Road colleagues eager to hear word for word the latest encounter between the inspector and the pathologist. So far, this one had been a disappointment. Maybe, hoped the sergeant, the comment would at last give him something to recount. Maybe Blizzard would rise to the bait like he always did. The inspector didn't.

'Any idea where the drugs are coming from?' asked Reynolds when it became clear that his ploy had failed. 'You had a chemist broken into?'

'Not for two months,' said the inspector. 'We're checking the rest of the city.'

'And, of course, you ruled out the pharmacy here,' said Reynolds, giving the inspector another mischievous look. 'Indeed, I understand you might be off the administrator's Christmas card list as a result of the somewhat indelicate nature of your inquiries. The words 'bull' and 'china shop' spring readily to mind, Inspector.'

'He did express some dissatisfaction with my comments, as I recall,' said Blizzard blandly; he was not in the mood for confrontation with the pathologist.

'The man's a buffoon, if you ask me,' said Reynolds. 'What's that phrase you use? A stuffed shirt? Mind, if you tell anyone that I agreed with you on something then I would have to kill you.'

'So kind,' murmured Blizzard.

There was silence for a few moments then Reynolds lowered his voice.

'Look, you did not get this from me,' he said, looking at the inspector, 'but I would not rule the pharmacy out of your thinking too quickly this time around. There have been rumours.'

'Rumours? What rumours?' said Blizzard.

'That someone linked to the pharmacy is getting drugs out for sale on the black market. That it started when the Hennessey girl fell ill.'

'Yes, but our drugs squad checked out all the staff last time,' said the inspector.

'Then perhaps you need to look deeper. Not that I am telling you how to do your job, Inspector.'

The comment finally irked Blizzard.

'There can be a danger in attaching too much significance to gossip, you know,' he said testily.

'But surely your job is based on gossip?'

Reynolds gave him a sly look. 'I believe they even have a phrase for it now — intelligence-led policing — although it does rather make me wonder what you were using before. Lack of intelligence, presumably.'

Blizzard glowered at him.

'Besides, I'm just telling you what I heard,' Reynolds gave a slight smile. 'Are you going to do anything about it?'

'So far all you have given me is idle gossip.'

'Fair enough. Oh, before I forget, how is Miss Hennessey? I understand you went to see her.'

'How on earth do you know that?'

'Gossip,' said Reynolds with a smile. 'Hospitals don't have many secrets, Inspector.'

'Point taken,' said Blizzard grudgingly, inwardly furious that he had allowed himself to be outmanoeuvred. 'I'll look at the pharmacy again.'

'Thank you,' said Reynolds, looking down at the young man's body. 'Who is doing the ID on Bobby?'

'We've got someone bringing the parents in.'

'Well, I hope whoever it is has treated them with respect. This will be an awfully difficult time for them, you know.'

'I am sure Detective Constable Ellis will

have acted entirely appropriately.'

'Why would you think any different?' said Reynolds, glancing at Colley and giving the merest of winks.

Noticing the gesture, again, Blizzard held his tongue and looked across at the sergeant, who shrugged. There was a light knock on the door and in walked a young blonde woman. Five foot eight and slim with short, slightly waved hair, Detective Constable Fee Ellis was twenty-nine and, having graduated from university, had served as a uniformed officer on the east side of the city before being moved to Western CID. The daughter of a retired detective sergeant, with whom Blizzard had worked briefly in his early days, Fee had been the inspector's girlfriend for the best part of two years. Colleagues were now openly speculating about the possibility of marriage but, having gone through an acrimonious divorce as a young man, it was taking a long time for Blizzard to acclimatize to the idea.

As ever when they were working together, the two officers assumed a professional air.

'How are the parents?' asked Blizzard.

'In bits. They had no idea he was using drugs.'

Blizzard glanced over her shoulder to where a couple were standing at the far end of the corridor, the man supporting the sobbing woman, an arm around her shoulders. She seemed close to collapse.

'I'll have a word,' said the inspector. He walked over to them. 'Mr and Mrs Leyton?'

The man nodded, the woman said nothing.

'I am DCI Blizzard. I am investigating the death of your son.'

The man nodded but again the woman said nothing, her body racked by sobs.

'I know this is difficult for you,' said Blizzard, 'but I must ask a couple of questions. Did you know that Bobby was taking drugs?'

'We had no idea,' replied the father, his voice little more than a whisper. 'None at all. Who sold them to him, Inspector? Who would do a thing like this?'

'That's what we are trying to find out.'

'Well, it's taking you a long time,' said the woman, breaking free of her husband's hold and staring at the inspector, anger flashing in her eyes. 'Bobby is the second, isn't he? How many young lives, Inspector! How many?'

She stared expectantly at Blizzard, who did not reply; he was not sure what to say in the face of her anger. He had never been good at empathy, normally left that to others. When he realized that Colley and Ellis were still in the mortuary room, talking to Reynolds,

Blizzard produced what he imagined was a compassionate look.

'We are trying our best, we really are,' he said, but realized the moments the words came out that they sounded lame; it struck him that a lot had sounded lame over the past twenty-four hours.

'Well, your best is not good enough!' spat the mother.

'Come on, love,' said the man, putting an arm round her shoulders. 'I am sure the chief inspector is doing everything in his power to catch this person.'

'He's not doing a very good job!' cried the mother, wrenching free from her husband's hold and glaring at the inspector.

Hearing the raised voice, Colley and Ellis came to stand next to Blizzard. Something about their presence seemed to calm the mother down and, her anger spent, she allowed her husband to put his arm around her again.

'You mentioned Lorraine,' said the sergeant. 'Did Bobby know her?'

'They both went to Queen Mary's.'

'The sixth form college?'

'Yes. They took some of the same subjects,' nodded the father.

Peter Reynolds, who had been standing at the door to the mortuary, now stepped into the corridor.

'Gordon,' he said, walking up to the father and touching him lightly on the arm, 'I am so sorry about this but would you be able to identify your son now?'

The father nodded and he and his wife walked slowly into the room. Blizzard watched them go then turned round to face the other detectives.

'She's right,' he said grimly. 'Our best has not been good enough.'

His mobile phone rang. The inspector fished the device out of his jacket pocket and listened in silence to the person on the other end. With a muttered 'thank you' he turned to look at the officers again.

'In fact,' he said quietly, 'it's been nowhere near good enough.'

10

'Now we really are in trouble,' said Blizzard, as he stared down at the body of the teenaged girl lying on the edge of the copse.

The inspector turned round to look at Colley but the sergeant said nothing. He did not need to; his appalled expression said it all. It was late morning and the officers were standing on the fringes of a school playing field. The call that had summoned them had come from the shocked head teacher at the city's girls' school, which stood in one of Hafton's most affluent areas, surrounded by tree-lined avenues and detached houses with deep drives. The body had been found by a group of pupils heading out onto the field during their mid-morning break. It had not taken them long to recognize the dead girl as a former pupil.

Blizzard turned round and gloomily surveyed the field. Ice glistened on the grass and the sharp winter sun dappled the trees. In other circumstances, thought Blizzard, it would have been a beautiful scene, especially after the freezing fog and snow flurries that had so blighted recent days. The re-emergence of the sun should have been a welcome event but the presence of the dead girl ensured that the sensation was exactly the opposite. Letting his gaze range over to the Edwardian school building thirty metres away, Blizzard saw a gaggle of staff gathering outside one of the side doors. Behind them he could see, through classroom windows, girls straining for a better view.

Blizzard returned his silent attention to the dead girl and the officer crouched down by the body, Detective Inspector Graham Ross, divisional head of forensics at Abbey Road. Gone was the normal banter between Blizzard and the man he usually called Versace because of his immaculate appearance; this morning, Ross's brown wavy hair was as beautifully groomed as ever, there was not a suspicion of stubble on his face and he was dressed in a pressed, grey, designer suit with a blue silk tie. His gleaming black shoes were flecked with drops of water from the grass. Blizzard glanced down at his own scuffed brogues — whatever the situation, he always did the same thing when he was with Ross, had tried to stop doing so for years but still couldn't resist the instinct. Normally, the gesture would have brought about amused looks from other officers — but not this morning.

'So what we got, Graham?' asked Blizzard.

'This,' said the DI, reaching down beside the body and producing a plastic shopping bag, which clinked. He peered inside. 'Pop bottles. One of them's half full.'

'Any idea what they are?'

'Do you need to ask?'

'I suppose not,' sighed Blizzard. 'The Press will have a field day with this, you know. I take it there's no chance she died of anything else?'

'It doesn't look like she has been injured.'

'The head teacher reckons she's called Charlotte Grayson,' said Colley. 'Anything to confirm that?'

'I'll check,' said Ross, reaching into the girl's jacket pocket.

'What do we know about her?' asked Blizzard, turning to his sergeant.

'Parents reported her missing last night. She'd told them she was at a friend's, doing homework, but when it got to past ten, they became worried and rang the friend, who knew nothing about it. Whatever Charlotte Grayson had planned, it wasn't homework.'

'Please tell me that we did something about the parents' call when it came in,' said Blizzard. 'There have already been enough foul-ups on this one.'

'Control asked uniform to keep an eye out. Clearly that was not enough.'

'Nothing has been enough,' said Blizzard grimly.

'Not sure that's entirely fair, guv,' said Ross. 'Teenagers go missing all the time. I don't know where my Rachel is half the time and she's only fourteen. You think you know them, but in the end you just take their word for it that they're where they say they are. When you see something like this happen, it's scares the life out of you.'

'Got that ID?' asked Blizzard.

'Provisional driving licence,' said Ross, producing the document from the girl's pocket and reading the first sheet. 'It's definitely Charlotte Grayson. Jesus, what a waste, she only turned seventeen a fortnight ago.'

'What's her address?' asked Blizzard.

Ross glanced down at the licence.

'The Laurels in Jasmine Avenue,' he said. 'Isn't that the big one on the corner — the one behind those high walls?'

'I investigated a burglary there four or five years ago,' nodded Colley. 'Really swish place — huge heated swimming pool, massive garden, Bentley in the front drive. Not exactly the kind of place you'd expect to see a junkie.'

'God, I hate these kind of crimes,' said Ross, standing up. 'In my experience, those kind of parents always refuse to believe that their little darlings would do anything illegal.'

'Perhaps they'd be right,' said Colley, looking down at the girl's body. 'Maybe it *was* the first time she'd taken drugs. Maybe she was experimenting. You just hope when someone offers yours something that they're able to resist the temptation, that they are savvy enough to . . . well, you know . . . '

His voice tailed off; everyone knew what he was thinking. Ever since the birth of his daughter, the sergeant had voiced such concerns more and more.

'Anything else on her?' asked the inspector.

The forensics officer reached back into the pocket.

'A Students' Union card,' he said. 'Care to guess where she went after leaving this place?'

'I think we can all guess that,' said Blizzard. He turned to Colley. 'We need to take a closer look at Queen Mary's. Its name is cropping up too often for comfort.'

The sergeant was about to reply when he noticed Blizzard looking beyond him and turned to follow the inspector's gaze. Ross came to join them and all three watched Peter Reynolds walking across the field towards them, carrying a battered black bag.

'Can anyone hear the flapping of wings?' murmured Blizzard.

'Guv?' said Ross.

'The Angel of Death has descended into our midst.'

Colley and Ross exchanged amused glances; despite the grim nature of the circumstances, an encounter between Blizzard and Reynolds was always to be relished.

'Some might say, Inspector,' said Reynolds, as he walked up to them, 'that one dead teenager in a morning is misfortune but that two ranks as sheer carelessness.'

'What happened to respect?' grunted Blizzard, as Reynolds ambled over to the body, knelt down and unclipped his bag. 'Surely poor Charlotte Grayson deserves that, just as much as Bobby Leyton.'

'Maybe so,' said Reynolds with the merest of smiles, 'but I did not know Charlotte Grayson — and I certainly do not know her family. Her father is not, to the best of my knowledge, a member of my golf club.'

Blizzard wondered if it was the done thing to murder a pathologist.

'Does it look like the others?' he asked instead. 'Graham found a couple of bottles — in that bag.'

'You should know by now that I do not indulge in idle speculation.'

Even if wasn't the done thing to murder a pathologist, Blizzard decided, it would be worth it, if only for the sheer satisfaction it would give him. Colley and Ross saw the inspector's glowering expression and tried not to smile.

'Then perhaps,' said Blizzard, conscious that the group of teachers were still watching so trying to sound as civil as possible, 'you might hazard an educated guess?'

'Well,' said Reynolds, crouching down low over the body, 'there seems little evidence of injury. The body is extremely cold, but if she had been out all night that would be understandable. There was thick ice on my windscreen this morning so we cannot, I think, rule out hypothermia at this stage.'

'But drugs has got to be the best bet?'

Reynolds looked up and gave another of his smiles.

'I never bet,' he said.

Before Blizzard could reconsider the idea of murdering the pathologist, he saw Fee approaching across the grass, walking alongside a thin and somewhat sallow woman in her fifties.

'Mrs Gainsworthy,' explained the constable, when they reached the detectives, 'she's the head teacher here.'

'How can I help you, Mrs Gainsworthy?' asked Blizzard.

'I was wondering how long you would be

here?' The head teacher avoided looking at the body. 'It's very upsetting for the girls.'

'I imagine it is, but there are certain things we must do, as I am sure you can appreciate,' said Blizzard. 'We will be as quick as we can.'

He looked at Ross and the pathologist, who both nodded.

'While you are here,' said Blizzard. 'I believe that Charlotte Grayson was a former pupil of the school?'

'Yes, she was,' said the head teacher, still not looking at the body. 'Very good parents. This is a terrible tragedy.'

'Was there ever any suggestion that she was into drugs?'

'Drugs?' The headteacher looked shocked at the suggestion. 'Why on earth would you say that, Inspector?'

'It seems possible that Charlotte might have died after taking an overdose. I'm wondering if she might have started taking drugs when she was at your school.'

'We do not allow anything like that here.' The voice was icy cold, the contrast in the demeanour pronounced. Now Mrs Gainsworthy was on the defensive.

'I am sure you don't, but does it ever go on despite your insistence? I mean, teenagers will be teenagers.'

'Not here they won't and I really must

insist that you desist from this kind of speculation,' said the head teacher, assuming a voice that reminded Blizzard of his own schooldays. 'I find your comments most offensive and uncalled for. Even if poor Charlotte had taken drugs, she was no longer a pupil of this school so it's nothing to do with us.'

'I'm not sure that necessarily follows.'

'I really would ask that you do not repeat these kind of suggestions further afield,' said the head teacher. 'The parents of our girls pay a considerable amount of money for their children to come here and such a suggestion would be exceedingly damaging to our reputation. Exceedingly damaging.'

'Yes, but surely it is more important to — '

'I really must insist. And might I also ask that you remove Charlotte's body as soon as possible, please? This is, obviously, a most unfortunate event but Charlotte had already left the school and I really would not like her to stay here any longer than is absolutely necessary.'

With Blizzard rendered speechless, she turned on her heel and stalked back towards the school.

'I wonder what Ofsted would say about her pastoral care?' murmured Colley.

'Like I said,' remarked Ross, 'I hate these

kind of investigations. These people think they own you.'

'I must say,' said Reynolds, coming to stand next to the inspector, 'you really do have a most remarkable way with witnesses, Blizzard. Really most remarkable indeed. I would even go as far as to suggest that it is a gift.'

Blizzard glowered at him and was about to reply when he saw a fresh-faced uniformed officer walking briskly across the field, passing the head teacher as he approached the detectives. Blizzard was struck by how young he looked.

'Jesus Christ,' murmured the inspector. 'I must be getting old.'

'Sir,' said the young constable as he arrived at the copse. 'There's a journalist at the front gate. Bloke from the local rag. Says he wants to talk to you.'

'Tell him to crawl back under his stone.'

'He's very insistent, refuses to go away.'

'Then arrest him.'

The constable looked confused.

'You do know how to arrest someone, I take it?' said Blizzard archly.

'Yes, of course, sir, but on what charge?'

'Being a journalist. I don't know, make something up.' Noticing the officer's uncomfortable expression, Blizzard sighed. 'Come on.'

As Reynolds watched them walk across the field, he looked at two detectives.

'How on earth do you work with him?' asked the pathologist. 'The man is insufferable.'

'You should see him when he's in a bad mood,' said Colley. 'Then he can be quite tetchy.'

Blizzard accompanied the uniformed officer across the field, skirting past the school building and ignoring the huddle of teachers and the girls standing up at the nearest classroom window. Walking down the front path, he saw another constable standing at the gate with a man in his early twenties. Blizzard did not recognize the journalist and glanced suspiciously at his T-shirt and jeans and his unshaven face.

'I'm on a day off,' explained the reporter, noticing the inspector's expression.

'Then how did you find out about this?'

'I live over there,' said the reporter, gesturing to a row of detached houses. 'The one with the BMW parked out front.'

'They're paying you too much,' grunted Blizzard.

'It's my dad's. I still live at home with my parents. Can't afford anything else on a reporter's wage. Look, are you going to tell me what's happening here, Chief Inspector? I saw Peter Reynolds arrive a few minutes ago. I assume it's a body.'

'We're not really in a position to — '

'Come on, Chief Inspector, don't do the no comment thing with me. I know something's cracking off.'

'Maybe you do, sunshine,' said Blizzard curtly, 'but nevertheless I am still not prepared to give you the satisfaction of — '

'Is it another one?'

'Another one?' said Blizzard sharply. 'What do you mean by that?'

'I heard there was a young man found last night,' explained the reporter. 'Off Cross Street. Drug-related, they reckon.'

'Who reckons?'

'My newsdesk.'

'And how do they know about it?' said Blizzard. 'We haven't put anything out about it yet.'

'So there is something cracking off then?'

'Yes, and I want to know how you know about it,' said the inspector suspiciously.

'When I rang in to see if the desk knew what was happening down here, they said someone had spotted your lot on the wasteland off Cross Street early this morning. Said you had taped off an area and locals reckoned there was a teenager's body. Are the two incidents linked?'

'It's a bit more complicated than that.'

The reporter gestured to the school building.

'It is something to do with this place?' he asked. 'The headteacher won't like it if it is. Don't think dead bodies fit in with her world view.'

'I'm sure,' said Blizzard. Something made him turn round to follow the reporter's gaze. The head teacher was staring at him from one of the ground floor windows. Her harsh words a few minutes before came back to him and he nodded. 'Well, I am afraid to say that the girls' school is right in the middle of it. Right in the middle. Tell me, son, when's your deadline?'

'Twelve-thirty for the main city edition. Mind, that's pushing it.'

'Well, young man,' said Blizzard, glancing at his watch, 'it looks like you've got yourself an exclusive.'

11

Half an hour later, John Blizzard was sitting in an armchair in the living room of a detached house on one of Western's more pleasant housing estates. Sitting on the sofa was a bespectacled middle-aged man with his arm round a sobbing woman. Blizzard glanced across at Heather Morrison, who was sitting on the other armchair. A slim brunette in her early thirties, the head of Abbey Road drugs squad was wearing a dark suit which seemed appropriate for the sombre occasion. Blizzard gave the slightest of nods.

'I am sorry about this,' said Morrison quietly, 'but we really do have to ask some questions. I know it's difficult but we need to know who sold Charlotte the dr — '

'Do you have any children?' interrupted the father.

The question startled Morrison.

'No,' she said. 'No I do not.'

'Then you cannot know how we are feeling.' The comment was laced with anger. 'You just cannot even start to understand what we are going through.'

'Yes, I appreciate that but — '

'Please.' The voice was trembling. Pleading. 'Please just go.'

'We are sorry,' said Blizzard, standing up, 'we'll come back later.'

As the DCI reached the door, followed by a surprised Heather Morrison, Charlotte Grayson's father took his arm away from his wife and stood up.

'Mr Blizzard,' he said.

Blizzard turned to look at him.

'Don't come back to this house unless you have arrested whoever did this,' said the father, his resolve beginning to weaken as tears forced their way to the surface. 'Just you don't.'

Blizzard turned on his heel and walked from the room. Out in the street, he turned to Heather Morrison.

'Enough,' he said.

'What?' Morrison was startled by the ferocity of the comment.

'Enough,' said Blizzard again.

★ ★ ★

'Three young lives,' said Blizzard, jabbing a finger on the photographs pinned on the board. 'Look hard at the young people on those pictures, ladies and gentlemen, because we have failed them. We have let them all down and we have let their families down.'

He let his gaze roam round the room — a trick he had learnt from George Moore — allowing it to settle on each of the dozen detectives in turn. A challenge to each and every one of them. It was 1.30 p.m. and the officers were gathered in the CID squad room at Abbey Road. Among them was Colley, perched on the windowsill. At the desks in front were other CID officers, including Chris Ramsey and Fee Ellis, sitting next to Graham Ross. On the other side of the room were half-a-dozen drugs squad officers, including Heather Morrison, who made little secret of her irritation at the inspector's comments, frowning and glancing round at her colleagues for support. She did not look at the photographs of the teenagers but everyone else in the room did; at Lorraine Hennessey's smiling face, her blonde hair blowing in the wind as she stood on a seafront; at Bobby Leyton's more serious features as he held up a certificate won in a school art competition just before he left to go college; at Charlotte Grayson, a slim brunette standing in front of a medieval castle, the picture taken on a family holiday the previous summer. Several officers shifted uncomfortably in their seats, but not Heather Morrison.

'With due respect, guv,' she said, unable to contain herself any longer, 'I think your comments are out of order. Well out of order.'

'I'll tell that to Charlotte Grayson's parents when we go back, shall I?' Blizzard stared angrily at her. 'Perhaps her father will apologize for kicking us out. And I'm sure Bobby Leyton's mother will feel much better when she realizes that we have done a cracking job.'

'That's not fair, guv,' protested Morrison. 'We've done everything we can to solve this one. You know that.'

'Do I?' asked Blizzard, fixing her with a steely look. 'Do I really, Detective Inspector? In which case then, would you kindly tell me who supplied the drugs to these kids?'

Blizzard tapped his hand on the board then looked hard at her again.

'Give me a name,' he said, 'and I'll happily take it all back. In fact, we can nip out and arrest them now, if you like.'

'Well, we do not know that yet but — '

'But nothing. Whichever way you view it, this is failure. Abject failure and two kids dead because of it.' Noticing Morrison's expression, Blizzard softened his tone. 'Look, Heather, I am not blaming you. I am not blaming anyone. I am just saying that despite our best efforts, we still have no idea who's pushing the stuff to these kids and now we have two deaths on our hands — three, when they turn Lorraine's life support off. That's carnage, whichever way you look at it.'

Blizzard glanced at the clock on the wall.

'Pretty soon,' he said, 'the evening paper will hit the streets with a story about what has happened. I have authorized the article because we need public help on this one. When the paper appears, folks will be demanding to know what we are doing about it. Parents will be terrified that their kid could be next. Shit, I'm terrified that their kid could be next.'

Ross nodded in agreement.

'So,' continued Blizzard, 'we will have to give them some answers and quickly — and we need them yesterday. In fact, if we'd had them yesterday, those two kids might not be dead.'

'Do I assume that you have now taken over the case?' said Morrison coldly. 'Have I been removed from the inquiry?'

'Obviously, you and your team will still be working on the investigation — we need your expertise — but what it needs is a new approach, Heather. New thinking.'

'With all due respect, sir, that's easy for you to say, but we've gone back to half-a-dozen informers since those kids were found and come up with nothing.' Morrison glanced around at her officers, who nodded their agreement. 'Whoever is supplying these drugs is a new kid on the block.'

'Well they would appear to be at it again,' said Blizzard. 'And it seems to me that the sixth form college is the place to start. All three of our kids attended classes there.'

The inspector nodded at Colley, who walked to the front of the room and pinned a photograph of a large Victorian building on the board, next to those of the three young people. The detectives looked for a few moments at the three-storey red-brick frontage with its gothic-style towers and turrets and tiny top-floor attic windows.

'For those who do not know,' said Colley, 'this pile is Queen Mary's Sixth Form College. It stands in Queen's Drive and dates from 1871 — '

'1872, actually,' interrupted Blizzard. 'It was built as a family home for Sir Esmund Jacobs, one of the city's early railway pioneers.'

'Right,' said Colley, who had never shown any interest in Blizzard's fascination with the city's industrial history. 'Anyway, these days, it is home to two hundred and fifty students, virtually all of them drawn from the city's more affluent areas. Our three kids, for example, all came from good families: Bobby's parents run a company supplying top of the range bathrooms, Lorraine's dad is a sales director, Mum is a lawyer, and Charlotte's father is a company secretary.'

Colley gave a slight smile.

'It will not surprise you to learn that I did not go to Queen Mary's,' he said. 'They didn't do O-Level dicking about.'

The joke eased the tension and even Heather Morrison relaxed a little. Blizzard let the laughter ripple round the room, appreciating as so often the sergeant's ability to dissipate tension with his sense of humour.

'It is my belief,' continued Colley, serious again, 'that the nature of the college is important because kids from those kind of middle-class families can be somewhat naïve in their approach to life. Too much Warhammer.'

More laughs.

'Thank you, Sergeant,' said Blizzard, walking up to the board and waiting for Colley to resume his place at the window, 'this isn't the Royal Variety Show. However, David is right. Some of these kids are easy prey for someone with a bit of street nous. That's one of the reasons I reckon our dealer has strong links with the place. Easy pickings. What did you find last time, Heather?'

'The odd bit of cannabis, as you would expect, but nothing heavier than that.'

'Then we try again — and if that means we interview every student at the place, then we do it.'

'But there are two hundred and fifty of them,' protested Morrison. 'It would take ages.'

'And even that is not as long as Bobby Leyton or Charlotte Grayson will be dead,' replied Blizzard, giving her a sharp look. 'Let's not forget what's happened here, Inspector.'

Morrison frowned but stayed silent.

'Hopefully, our task will be made less onerous with the college's co-operation,' said Blizzard and looked at Colley. 'They've agreed to let us see their files. David, did you ask the girls' school head teacher to do the same?'

'Yes, but she said she would have to consult her governors first. Said she did not want her school dragged into the investigation.'

'Let's hope she does not read the paper then,' said Blizzard. 'Tell her that her time has run out. I don't want some stuck-up head teacher mucking us about. You can tell her I said that as well.'

'Thanks for that,' said Colley gloomily.

'Right,' said Blizzard, 'we also have to find

out where they are getting the gear from. Anyone got any bright ideas?'

'Got to be a chemist's,' said Ross.

'There's another option though, isn't there?' said Ramsey, speaking for the first time in the briefing. 'Maybe we were wrong to rule out the General Hospital's pharmacy last time.'

'Yes but we checked every person who works there as well,' said Morrison, still with a defensive tone in her voice. 'And every one of them came up clean.'

'So we check again,' said Blizzard. 'Look, I know you are not enjoying this, Heather, but we need to regard it as a new investigation.'

He was about to continue when Arthur Ronald appeared at the door. He walked over to take a seat in the corner of the room.

'Don't mind me,' he said.

'Chris was just asking if we should take another look at the hospital pharmacy,' said Blizzard.

'You'll need something new then,' said Ronald. 'I have just come off the phone from a friend of mine, a consultant at the hospital. He reckons the hospital is in line for a fifteen million pound expansion and the administrator is twitchy about any bad publicity. Apparently, there was a hospital down south lost its money when there was a negative

116

story in the local press.'

'Surely a murder investigation is more important?' said Ramsey.

'Maybe so, Chris, but my friend reckons the administrator is even prepared to go for an injunction to stop us going in there without evidence. Mind, I'm open to suggestions.'

'Maybe we put someone in undercover,' suggested Ramsey.

'Not so sure,' said Ronald, pursing his lips. 'The administrator is a sharp cookie. He'd be bound to see right through it. Could be time for Plan B.'

The superintendent looked at Blizzard.

'Do we have a Plan B?'

'At this rate,' said Blizzard, 'I'm not even sure we have a plan A.'

A young woman walked into the briefing room and looked at Blizzard.

'They're ready,' she said.

'Marvellous,' replied the inspector, heading for the door. 'Absolutely bloody marvellous.'

12

'So is the story true?' asked one of the reporters, holding up the evening newspaper.

TEENAGERS' DEATHS LINKED TO DRUGS, screamed the headline next to a picture of officers guarding the wasteland at Cross Street. The second picture on the page showed two uniformed officers standing at the front gates of the girls' school and below it a small library headshot of Blizzard.

From his vantage point behind a desk at the front of the Abbey Road briefing room, the inspector looked at the gathered journalists. Two television cameras were filming him and a couple of radio reporters were recording his comments. There was also a smattering of newspaper reporters. Blizzard sighed; he hated press conferences and had always detested dealing with journalists, but he had also long realized that if you wanted to get a message out then the media was the only way to do it. And instinct told him that he was going to need all the help he could get on this one. Blizzard glanced over to the back of the room where Chris Ramsey and Colley were leaning against the wall, next to Arthur

Ronald. The superintendent looked worried; he always experienced the same sensation when witnessing the latest encounter in Blizzard's turbulent relationship with the media.

'Yes,' said Blizzard, noticing the young newspaper reporter among the crowd, now dressed in a shirt and tie, 'yes, the story is absolutely true. A very accurate piece of reporting.'

The young reporter caught his eye, hoping for some kind of recognition, but Blizzard did not acknowledge his presence; he had long since refused to develop personal relationships with journalists.

'I think our press officer has handed out a summary of what has happened,' continued Blizzard, 'but if anyone has anything else they would like to ask, now would be the time.'

The questions came hard and fast.

'Have you confirmed that drugs caused these teenagers' deaths?' asked another reporter, glancing down at the newspaper in his hand. 'This piece says you are waiting for test results.'

'We are, but for the moment drugs seem the most likely cause.'

'Do you know what drugs were involved?'

'We are not confirming that yet, although I can say that we believe we are dealing with prescription drugs.'

'Does that mean you are linking these deaths with what happened to Lorraine Hennessey?' asked a reporter.

'Yes.'

'Would you care to elaborate?'

'I can confirm it is one line of inquiry.'

'Do you believe the same person supplied the drugs?'

'It is something we are looking at very seriously.'

'Do you believe the girls' school is involved? I mean, Charlotte Grayson was found there and, according to this article, she was a former pupil.'

'Again, it is one line of inquiry. However, all three of the three young people also attended Queen Mary's Sixth Form College as well and we will be concentrating some of our efforts there.'

'So does that mean you think the drugs were supplied by one of the students?'

'No comment.'

'Do you have a message for whoever did sell these drugs?'

Blizzard had been waiting for this moment; he had been playing the game long enough to know that the journalists were always after a good quote, a sound-bite that would play well.

'Yes,' he said, adopting his most serious expression. 'The deaths of these two young people is a tragedy. They have been cut down when they had their lives ahead of them and we are determined to bring those responsible to justice. Someone in this city knows who is supplying those drugs, may even be wrestling with their conscience as I speak. It may be possible that that person did not intend those poor young people to die. I would appeal to that person to come forward. Believe me, it will be easier for them if they come to us than if we knock on their door.'

After a few more questions, which the inspector swatted away easily, he stood up.

'Well, thank you for your time, ladies and gentlemen . . . ' he began.

'Before you go,' said one of the reporters. 'Do you not feel a sense of responsibility that this has happened again? Guilt maybe?'

Blizzard stared at him.

'Guilt?' he said quietly. 'And what exactly do you mean by that?'

'Well, Lorraine Hennessey was a year ago and you still have not made an arrest on that one. Now two more teenagers are dead. I mean, how does that make you feel, Chief Inspector? You've failed these kids, haven't you?'

Blizzard glanced across the room at

121

Ronald, who was pursing his lips; it was the question the superintendent had dreaded. The question they had all dreaded. The superintendent glanced at Ramsey and Colley, who both shrugged. Everyone knew it was impossible to predict Blizzard's reactions when faced with the media; it normally did not take much provocation for him to lose his cool. The media knew that, knew that his reactions often provided added spice to a story. For a few moments, there was a tense silence in the room as Blizzard stared hard at the journalist who had asked the question. The reporter tried to retain eye contact for a few moments but looked away under the inspector's searing gaze.

'How does it make me feel?' said Blizzard eventually, an edge to his voice. 'How do you think it makes me feel, son? I mean, how would you feel?'

Ronald closed his eyes. The reporter did not reply, taken aback by the calmness of the inspector's demeanour and the ferocity of his gaze.

'I was just asking a question,' said the journalist somewhat weakly.

'Well, here is the answer,' said Blizzard, his voice ominously quiet so that those on the back row had to strain to hear it, 'and you make sure you write it down. Make sure you all write it down. Any death is upsetting for police officers, but when it is young people it is even more so and this case is no exception.'

He glanced across at Colley.

'Many of our officers are parents themselves,' continued the inspector. 'I myself recently became a godparent and you can take it from me, we will all be doing everything in our power to bring this person to book. They have taken away the lives of young people who had everything to live for. Whoever did this will not go unpunished. That's a promise.'

There was silence for a few moments. Ronald opened his eyes and gave a small sigh of relief. Next to him, Chris Ramsey gave a nod of approval and glanced at Colley, who smiled slightly.

'Thank you,' said the journalist, sitting down with a relieved look on his face.

'Now,' said Blizzard, heading for the door, 'myself and my team have a lot of work to do, as I am sure you can appreciate. Should you have any other queries, Gaynor from our press office can help, I am sure. She's the young lady standing at the back of the room. She will be delighted to assist you in any way she can.'

And with that he strode from the room.

★ ★ ★

David Colley took a deep breath and walked into the head teacher's office at the girls' school. Mrs Gainsworthy was sitting behind the desk and eyed his arrival without enthusiasm.

'Is this any of your doing?' she asked, picking up the newspaper, holding it with the tips of her fingers as if it were dirty. 'My school plastered all over the front page of the local rag?'

'Ah, no. No, it wasn't.'

'I assume it was that Blizzard man,' said the head teacher throwing the newspaper across the table in the sergeant's direction. 'Well, you can tell your chief inspector that his actions are disreputable and unbecoming of someone in his — '

'Mrs Gainsworthy,' said Colley, cutting across her, 'I really don't have time for this. If you want to talk to the DCI, I can give you his number. In the meantime, I need to see the files on all your current students and those who have left within the past three years.'

'I thought I made it clear that I would have to consult my governors over this. We cannot just decide to — '

'I am afraid we do not have time to wait for their decision.'

She glared at him and reached over to pick up the newspaper.

'Do you know how badly this story will have damaged the reputation of this school?' she said bitterly. 'Just because one of our former students was stupid enough to take drugs.'

'I would have thought that finding who killed her is more important than reputations,' said Colley, an edge to his voice.

The head teacher's demeanour changed, her anger replaced by something more vulnerable. She seemed close to tears. Colley watched the transformation with surprise.

'You must think me a most callous woman, Sergeant,' she said quietly.

'I'm sorry?'

'You must think me callous — appearing to care more about the reputation of the school than these poor young people.'

'I didn't think that for a — '

'Oh, yes you did. And who can blame you?' She placed the newspaper back on the desk, taking great care that it was straight. 'Do you know how hard I have worked to build up the reputation of this school?'

'No, I do — '

'When I came here ten years ago, it was in an awful state. Standards slipping, poor inspection reports, low morale among staff. I have worked so hard to turn it round, I really have. It has been exhausting, so exhausting.'

'Yes, I am sure you . . .'

'I sometimes think that outsiders do not realize the pressures that go with being a head teacher at a school like this,' she said, interrupting him again. 'Tell me, did you have pushy parents when you were at school, Sergeant?'

'Er, no,' said Colley, with a smile. 'To be honest, I'm not sure they knew where I was half the time. I was not the ideal teenage son. Bit of a scallywag.'

'I'm sure you were,' she said, returning the smile. 'Perhaps you were lucky, though. Parents at the other extreme can present their own problems. I will tell you something about Charlotte Grayson, Sergeant. When she was studying here, her mother came in at the end of every afternoon, demanding to know how much progress her daughter had made that day, wanting to see every bit of work she had done. It had been like that all through primary school as well.'

The head teacher gave a shake of the head.

'Madness.' She looked at the sergeant with a troubled expression on her face. 'I suppose that's why I was so funny with you and your Mr Blizzard. I think that what frightens me more than anything else is the idea that the pressure we put on our young people can drive them into the hands of drug dealers and their like. A rebellion, if you like. Sometimes we forget to let them just be kids. Of course we will help you, Sergeant Colley.'

She reached forward and pressed the button on the desk intercom.

'Janet,' she said, 'I am sending the sergeant back through. Please can you provide him with all the help he needs — and I mean all the help.'

'Ma'am?' The voice sounded surprised.

'You heard me. Whatever he asks for, let him have it.'

'Including the files?' said the disembodied voice.

'Yes, including the files.'

'But I thought the chair of governors was going to make the final decision, ma'am.'

'Somehow,' said the head teacher, giving the sergeant a half-smile, 'I think there are more important things than what Walter Jayston thinks.'

She stood up and reached out a hand.

'Good day, Sergeant,' she said. 'I hope you apprehend whoever did this, I really do.'

Colley shook the hand and walked out of the office, still trying to work out what he had done right.

13

Shortly after lunch, with her feet crunching on ice, Maureen Cox made her way up the uneven path leading through the allotments, glancing right and left as always at the make-do sheds, the winter sun glinting off roofs still piled high with snow. Even though this was Vic's world, Maureen loved her visits to the allotments; it was one of the few places where she had felt peace in recent years. She often felt that her visits had helped keep her sane. She knew that Vic would say the same, were he the kind of man to give voice to his feelings.

Returning her attention to the path ahead of her, she could only see one set of footprints, the marks of a boot that she instantly recognized. Almost reaching the top of the path, where the allotments gave way to a thin belt of trees before the housing estate began, Maureen turned right and pushed her way through a gate. It creaked slightly as it swung open.

'Need to get that oiled, Vic,' she said, as she always did.

There was no answer. Walking into the

allotment, she did not see her husband at first. Then she became aware of a presence and, turning to her left, saw him standing in front of his shed, staring out across the snow-covered beds with their meticulously planted and lovingly-tended rows of winter cabbages, sprouts and cauliflowers, the leaves glinting with a frost that had lingered for days.

'You'll not get much done today, love,' she said. 'You'll not get a spade through this for a start.'

He did not reply so she tried again.

'Ground will be rock hard, I should imagine, love.'

Her husband turned to look at her.

'Always find something to do,' he said.

Maureen studied him for a few moments. Dressed in an old grey overcoat and with a battered cap jammed across wispy grey hair, slightly stooped of stance and with sallow, sunken cheeks, it seemed to her that Vic Cox was a man growing old before her eyes. It had not always been like that; there had been a time when he was full of vigour and energy, a man with a love for life and a passion for the good things, for a night down the pub with friends and for long walks with the dog down by the river. All that had changed since his illness and today his decline seemed more pronounced than ever. Standing there in the chill of the allotment, Maureen could not shake the conviction that her husband was fading away. She'd seen it so many times before with her patients, had seen once-robust people hit so hard by illness that all their fight drained from them and they ended up doing nothing but waiting for death. Shadows, she called them. Shadows. She feared that the same was true of her husband and wondered now, as she wondered so many times, what she could do to change things.

'I brought you something to eat,' she said, trying to sound cheerful as she always did with him although, as ever, it came over sounding forced. She reached into her bag and produced a flask. 'Tomato soup. Your favourite. And some sandwiches as well. Ham.'

He nodded his thanks and took them from her.

'How long will you be here?' she asked.

He shrugged.

'Well don't forget I need that shelf fixing, love,' she said. 'It's hanging nearly off the wall. Don't want it falling onto the television. Not after we did all that saving to buy it.'

Vic did not acknowledge the comment and they stood in silence for a few moments, looking out across the allotment.

'You off in then?' he asked eventually, glancing at the nurse's uniform just visible beneath her open coat.

'Yes. I've left you something by the oven for tea. You'll need to turn it on about four. Give it twenty-five minutes. Oh, and don't forget to let the oven get up to temperature before you put it in. I've left some vegetables in a pan on the hob. They should only need ten minutes once the water's boiling.'

'Thanks,' said Vic and lapsed once more into silence.

Maureen wished she could say that it was a comfortable silence after all these years but it did not feel like that. Rather, it was a silence laden with sadness, she thought. Maureen sighed.

'I'll see you in the morning then,' she said and gave him a peck on the cheek.

'Aye,' he said, but did not kiss her in return.

She turned to go.

'Don't work too hard,' she said and pulled open the gate.

'Is he still alive?' he said, as she stepped out onto the path.

Maureen paused — she had expected the question — then walked back into the allotment.

'As far as I know, love,' she said.

He did not respond to the comment and Maureen walked out of the allotment again. A glance back showed that her husband had returned to his silent vigil, staring out over the allotment.

Maureen was still thinking about her husband as she stood next to the nurses' station at the far end of the ward more than two hours later. She was sipping a mug of tea, her first drink since getting in to start what already promised to be a busy shift, when she heard the buzzer at the main doors. She glanced up at the clock on the wall. 2.30 p.m. already. Reaching down to the button beneath the desk, she released the lock and watched as a stream of visitors appeared. For a few moments, she surveyed them. Despite more than thirty years in the job, she never failed to be fascinated by the picture they presented, some heavy of foot, dreading what they would find, others lighter of step, buoyed by a loved one's recovery, others, the first-timers, looking anxious as they walked down the corridor and read the names on the boards outside the side rooms. Maureen tensed as she recognized a familiar figure walking behind them. As the man neared, he caught sight of her.

'Maureen,' he said with a smile that was lacking in warmth. 'Well, well, long time no see.'

'Morris,' she said in a flat voice. 'I wondered when you'd turn up like a bad penny.'

'That's no way to talk to someone who's visiting an old friend, Maureen.'

'Some of your cronies came up to see him last night. Not exactly the best behaved.'

'I imagine they were maddened by grief.' Raynor did not even try to sound sincere. 'And your somewhat unpleasant reception left them deeply distressed.'

'I'm sure it did.' She gave him a curious look. 'Why all the interest in Harry Josephs anyway? What's he to you these days?'

'Oh, you know how it is, Maureen, we always look after our own. We're like one big family. Loyalty, it's a wonderful thing.' He gave a thin smile. 'Talking of happy families, how's Vic? Enjoying his retirement down the allotment?

Maureen Cox said nothing.

★ ★ ★

Back in Ronald's office at Abbey Road, the superintendent and Blizzard were sitting cradling mugs of tea. It was shortly after 3.30 and the first time either of them had been able to find any time to relax since the discovery of the bodies, both officers acutely aware that the early hours of a major inquiry were often the most important. Blizzard, who had been busy ensuring that his officers were properly deployed, was eating a sandwich.

'I didn't get chance to say,' remarked the superintendent, 'I thought you handled the press conference well. I've had run-ins with that reporter before.'

'Yeah, so have I. Next time I'll rip his balls off and use them for Christmas decorations.'

'Remind me to send you on that media relations training course,' murmured Ronald.

'Well, what do you expect me to say?' said Blizzard, taking a bite of sandwich. 'The man's a halfwit.'

'Maybe, but he did put into words what a lot of people will be thinking, not least the parents.'

'Yeah, I know, I know,' nodded Blizzard. 'In fact, I'm off to see Lorraine Hennessey's mother after she gets in from work. Taking Heather because she knows her. Not looking forward to it.'

'So where are we with all of this?' Ronald's expression betrayed his concern. 'We'll not be able to keep the Press at bay for long, they'll be demanding to see progress. We're already getting calls from worried members of the public, wondering if their kids are safe to go out. Control reckon they've had half a dozen calls already and front desk said at least three mums have turned up demanding answers. When are you getting the report back from Reynolds?'

'Tomorrow morning. Not that it matters, Ross has got a pretty good nose for these things and he's pretty sure that the methadone *was* spiked.'

'Anything else come in?' asked Ronald.

'Not much,' said the inspector, taking a final bite of sandwich and flicking crumbs off his trousers. 'We're doing door-to-door in the areas where the kids were found but we've not turned up anything yet. I've got Fee talking to both sets of parents again, see if they can provide us with anything else, but I'm not hopeful. None of them had even the remotest idea what their kids were up to.'

'Friends?'

'We're working our way through them but they're all pretty shocked — and if any of them do know where they got the drugs they're not saying. We're putting the fear of God into them, to make sure they're not tempted, but you know what kids are like.'

'Too true,' said Ronald gloomily. 'My son tried drugs once, you know.'

Blizzard looked at him in astonishment.

'Really?' he said. 'You never said anything before.'

'Would you?'

'Aye, I suppose. When did it happen?'

'Eighteen months ago. One of his mates had just turned sixteen and he had a party when his parents were out at a dinner. About eleven thirty, I get a call from the kid's dad to say he has just got back and found everyone trying to revive Mark after he collapsed in the bathroom.'

'Was he OK?'

'After a day or two. Turned out that he had been drinking strong lager all night and someone had given him a spliff. Turned his stomach.'

'He try it again?'

'Pretty sure he hasn't — it was such a horrendous experience for the lad.' Ronald gave Blizzard a thoughtful look. 'Just goes to show, mind, that there is only so much you can do. You see these newspaper headlines *Police officer's son convicted of drug offences* and you think 'there but for the grace of God'. If my lad hadn't taken so ill I would still not have known what happened. That's why we have to get this sorted and quickly, John. God knows how many other kids are being tempted by this new gear.'

'You're right about that,' said Blizzard, draining his mug and standing up.

'Could be time for that Plan B Ramsey was

on about,' said Ronald.

Blizzard's mobile phone rang.

'Hopefully,' he said, 'this is it.'

He listened to the call for a few moments then slipped the device back into his jacket pocket, a broad grin on his face.

'I think we can safely say that we have our Plan B,' he said. 'That was George Moore on a hospital payphone. Harry Josephs had a visitor this afternoon.'

'I thought I made it clear that he needs to take a back seat,' protested Ronald. 'This thing with the kids is much more important.'

'Au contraire,' said Blizzard, grabbing his jacket from the back of the chair and heading for the door. 'He might just be the key to it all. Come on, I'll explain on the way. Do you good to get out in the field, Arthur.'

'Where are we going?' asked a bemused Ronald.

'Time we went hospital visiting, I think,' said Blizzard. 'Hey, do you reckon accounts will let me claim a bunch of grapes on expenses?'

14

Heather Morrison sat in the wood-panelled room at Queen Mary's College and stared gloomily out of the window as the mid-afternoon darkness started once more to shroud the city. Already the street lights had flickered into life and the ice on the paths was glistening as the temperature once more began its downward spiral. The DI glanced up at the clock on the wall, looked back at the large pile of documents on the desk and sighed heavily. She had been sifting through the student files in the poorly lit room for more than two hours and had the beginnings of a headache.

The task felt like a punishment for past failings and for a woman who had always been deeply ambitious, it was not a pleasant feeling. It had also been, until recent events, an unusual sensation because Heather Morrison's career had been a highly successful one, furthered by a string of high-profile arrests in her early months as the first female officer in charge of Western Drugs Squad. The similarity with John Blizzard's career path had not gone unnoticed and there were those who had talked about her as a potential successor to him as head of divisional CID. There were those who believed that she could go even further and become the force's first female detective superintendent.

Then teenager Lorraine Hennessey was found slumped on a park bench not far from her home and everything changed. As days stretched into weeks without an arrest, then into months, Heather Morrison became aware that people had stopped talking about her as they had done previously. Instead, she knew that her abilities were being called into question for the first time in her glittering career. Sitting and staring out of the window now, she recalled Blizzard's briefing earlier that afternoon and her mind went back to the image of Lorraine Hennessey lying in her hospital bed. Heather realized with a stab of guilt that she had not been to see her for months.

She looked up as Colley walked into the room.

'Ah,' he said cheerily, gesturing to the pile of documents, 'the glamour of police work. How many you done?'

'A hundred and eleven.'

Colley winced.

'Ouch,' he said. 'Anything interesting?'

'The pile on the right is those who might

be worth a closer look, the others are the ones who would appear to be angels on earth.'

'Can't help noticing that the bad lads one is significantly smaller than the emissaries of the risen Lord,' said Colley, picking up the top folder from the lower of the two piles and opening it up. 'Edward Carrick. Why are you interested in him? He got form?'

'Hardly,' said Morrison with a rueful look. 'Our Edward did a remarkably detailed project on heroin smuggling for a geography project. Got him an A-plus and a special award from the principal. His drawing of an opium poppy was particularly commendable, apparently.'

'Jesus,' said Colley, tossing the file back down onto the table, 'we are in trouble.'

'Which is what I tried to tell Blizzard.' She hesitated; everyone knew that Colley was close to the DCI. 'Has he mentioned me at all?'

'No.'

Morrison looked hard at him but his expression gave nothing away.

'No,' she said, 'No, I don't suppose he has.'

* * *

Hospital visiting time was finished when Blizzard and Ronald arrived at Ward 46.

Maureen Cox was sitting at the far end of the corridor, a sheaf of medical files spread out on the desk, when she saw one of the nurses opening the door and engaging in conversation with the officers. When it went on for a couple of minutes without either of them moving from the door, Maureen frowned, got up from the nurses' station and walked down the corridor.

'I'll handle this, Alison,' she said, and the nurse disappeared into a side room. 'Mr Blizzard, I wondered when you would get here. I take it that this is official business?'

'I am afraid so, Sister.' Blizzard gestured to his colleague. 'This is Detective Superintendent Arthur Ronald. We would like to see George — in private if possible.'

'Because of Harry Josephs' visitor earlier this afternoon, I assume?'

'What makes you say that?' asked Blizzard.

'Because the moment he realized that he was here, George became very agitated and asked to make a phone call. We offered to wheel the machine over to the bed but he insisted on being taken out to the payphone on the landing. Said no one must hear.'

'He was calling me,' said Blizzard.

'So I gather.' Maureen fixed him with a beady stare. 'Are you going to tell me what's going on in my ward, Mr Blizzard? I do hope

141

that your visits to George over recent weeks have not been conducted with an ulterior motive in mind because if they have . . . '

'I come here out of friendship. I have known George for many years.'

'I am sure you have, but, given that he is an ex-copper, something tells me that your friendship is not the whole story. I would appreciate if you told me the bits I don't know.'

Blizzard hesitated.

'Oh, come on, Inspector,' said the sister. 'I wasn't born yesterday, you know. This afternoon's events have really upset George and if you are getting him into something connected to your work, that really is not a good thing at this stage of his recovery. A recovery which still remains fragile, might I add. You have a responsibility as a friend as well as a police officer. So, are you going to tell me what's happening?'

'I am not sure that I am at liberty to discuss police business.'

'If your business impinges on a patient's well-being, it becomes my business,' she said, an edge to her voice now. 'And around here, clinical need trumps everything else, even CID.'

Seeing Blizzard's confusion, her expression softened.

'Look,' she said, 'I really do need to know — if only for George's sake.'

'OK,' said the inspector, glancing at Ronald, who nodded. 'But can we go into a side room? I'd rather this did not become public knowledge, not at this stage anyway.'

Maureen led them into a small rest room behind the nurses' station and closed the door.

'So,' she said, gesturing for them to sit down in a couple of armchairs and waiting until they were settled, 'why is George so agitated?'

'He knows Harry Josephs from his time on the force,' said Blizzard. 'The man who came to see Harry this afternoon is called Morris Raynor. Most people know him as Morrie.'

'I have always called him Morris.'

'You know him?'

'I am afraid that I have not been entirely frank with you, Inspector.'

'I have yet to meet a person who has,' said the inspector. 'So what's your deep, dark secret, Sister Cox?'

'Myself and Morris go way back. Our mothers knew each other when we were little and she used to bring him round to play with me. Even then he was a bully.' She reached up and pulled back a flop of hair to reveal a small scar etched into her forehead. 'He did

143

that with a toy tractor.'

'Charming,' said Blizzard.

'We went to school together as well.' She shook her head. 'Bye, he was a nasty piece of work. Everyone was frightened of Morris Raynor.'

'Including you?'

'Maybe not everyone,' she said with a slight smile.

'I take it you did not keep in touch after school?'

'Our paths crossed occasionally. And yes, before you ask, I knew who Harry Josephs was the moment they brought him onto the ward. The Secrets Man.'

'You seem remarkably well informed on the machinations of the criminal fraternity, Sister,' said Ronald, looking closely at her. 'I'm intrigued — how might that be?'

'Look,' she said, lowering her voice, 'I'm not sure what this is about, but my experience of police officers is that they always find out about things eventually. If you are conducting some kind of investigation into Morris Raynor, I imagine that my part of the story will come out eventually. It's better that you hear it from me.'

'Go on,' said Blizzard.

'Back in the seventies, my husband ran a public house over on the east side,' said the sister, her features suggesting that she was attempting to control strong emotions. 'It was all Vic ever wanted to do. He had talked about it for years. He was an engineer by trade — they trained him when he did his National Service. Trouble is, the job was poorly paid and we never had much money. Never went anywhere more exotic than Blackpool for our holidays. 'Wait 'til I got that pub, princess,' he'd say. 'Things will be better then. We can go on holidays to Spain.' He was obsessed with Spain, was Vic. Anyway, when the factory hit hard times, he saw his redundancy money as his big chance.'

Her expression hardened.

'But it was ruined by Morris Raynor,' she said. The words were spat out, the venom surprising the detectives.

'What did he do?' asked Blizzard.

'Tried to make Vic pay protection money.'

'Sounds familiar,' murmured Ronald, glancing at Blizzard. 'What happened?'

'Usual story. I am sure I don't have to tell you that Morris Raynor ran the East side in those days. We had not been in the pub long, four or five days I think, when we were visited by three men just after we closed one night. Harry Josephs was one of them.'

'Harry handled a lot of that kind of thing for Raynor,' said Ronald. 'I think Morrie trusted him to keep folks in line.'

'Well, he was a coward,' said Maureen sharply. 'Always had a real yellow streak in him, did Harry, and this time, true to form, he turned up with two heavies and told Vic that if he did not pay up, they'd wreck the place.'

'What did your husband say to that?' asked Blizzard.

'Vic is as honest as the day is long, Inspector. And as proud as they come. He'd sunk everything into that place and there was no way he was going to give it all up just because some yobs told him to.'

'I take it he declined their offer then?' said Ronald.

'He wasn't that polite. I had never seen him so angry. He'd always been such a mild mannered man but he really lost it. Kicked them out into the street.'

'Not sure anyone does that to Morrie Raynor's men,' said Blizzard.

'No, they don't, Inspector, and Harry Josephs was as good as his word. He told Vic they would be back and two or three hours later we were in bed in the flat upstairs when they put all the pub's windows out. Every single one of them.'

'That was one of Raynor's favourite tricks,' nodded Ronald. 'I assume it worked?'

'Not immediately. Like I said, Vic was a stubborn man and he tried to keep going but when word got round that Morris Raynor was involved, folks stopped drinking there. No one wanted to risk falling foul of a man like that.'

Ronald and Blizzard nodded; they knew how Morrie Raynor operated.

'Vic did his best,' she said. 'Soldiered on for a few weeks but after the windows had gone out for the fourth time, he decided it was not worth the trouble and gave the place up. The insurance people were threatening to withdraw his cover. I remember the night he told me of his decision.'

She dabbed at her eyes with a handkerchief.

'Do you know what it's like to have your dream taken away?' she said. 'I had never seen him cry, not even when the kids were born, but he cried that night. Cried like a baby.'

The detectives said nothing and let her regain her composure once more. After thirty seconds, she began speaking again, her voice quiet.

'He was never the same after that,' she said.

'Did he get another pub?' asked Blizzard.

'He tried, but once word got out that he had crossed Morris Raynor, it never happened. We felt such outcasts — old friends would cross the street to avoid being seen with us. We ended up moving up to the north of the city and Vic got a job working at a supermarket, stacking shelves. He retired early on health grounds.' She shook her head again, tears closer than ever. 'It was like all the fight had gone out of him. He became a really quiet man, that's how I describe him to people now. A quiet man.'

The detectives let her compose herself once more.

'He's had multiple sclerosis for years,' she said. 'You can never prove anything but it started six months after we lost the pub. It's got really bad the last three or four years. Poor man, he's got so little strength in his arms these days. Can't even use a pair of secateurs on his allotment.'

'How old is Vic?' asked Ronald.

'He's only sixty-two.' Again, she shook her head sadly. 'It's no age. We had all these dreams of what we would do when we retired — I go next year, could go this year if we didn't need the money — but now, now I'm not sure that he'll last that long. Taking on that pub was the worst thing he ever did.'

'We used to work on the east side,' said Blizzard. 'Which pub was it?'

'The Kestrel.' She noticed their expressions. 'And before you ask, yes, the one where Des Fairley was murdered and no, Vic was

148

not the landlord when it happened. They'd all gone over to the Black Bull on Halter Street by then.'

'The one that burned down, as I recall,' asked Ronald.

'Funny that,' she said. 'Bad luck seemed to follow Morris Raynor around.'

'It certainly does,' said Blizzard. 'I take it you recognized him when he turned up this afternoon?'

'Had to do a double take, if I'm honest. I heard he'd had a really tough time in prison and it certainly looked like it. He looked different — older.'

'Don't we all,' murmured Blizzard.

'But nothing can change that horrible smile of his.'

Blizzard nodded; the showreel started to play again.

'We understand Harry Josephs had some other visitors,' said Ronald. 'The nurse who let us in — Nurse Ramage, I think she was called — said you seemed to know one of them.'

'Did she now?' murmured Sister Cox. 'What an observant girl she is. Yes, Harry had three visitors. A right rogue's gallery.'

'Which one of them did you know?'

'Geoff Bates.'

'What did they want?'

'To talk to Harry.'

'What about?' asked Blizzard.

'I don't know.'

'And you had them kicked out?'

'Like I said,' she said with a slight smile, 'clinical need trumps everything in here.'

'I take it you heard that Geoff Bates was murdered last night?' said Ronald.

'Heard it on the radio,' she nodded.

'Where do you know him from?'

'Bates was one the heavies that night in the pub. I recognized him the moment he turned up here. He might be older but his nose is pretty unmistakable.'

'Broke it in a pub brawl,' nodded Blizzard, sitting back in the chair and placing his hands behind his head. 'Well, well, Sister, you are a woman of infinite mystery, you really are.'

'And you would seem to be a man of mystery, Inspector.' She gave him a shrewd look. 'Do I assume that George is doing a bit of spying on Morris Raynor's cronies for you? You not satisfied with putting him behind bars once?'

Blizzard hesitated and glanced at Ronald.

'Oh, come on, Inspector,' she said, noticing the look. 'It doesn't take much working out. George keeps scribbling things down in a notebook in full view of everyone else then leaving the pages open when he falls asleep.

He's hardly Serpico.'

Blizzard raised his eyes to the ceiling and Ronald sighed.

'But if he is doing some work for you,' continued the sister, 'I would heartily recommend that he stops it immediately. Your friend has been very ill, I am sure you realize that, Inspector, and it would not take much to set him back on the decline again. I know that you and Morris Raynor have history, but you do have to think of your friend as well.'

Blizzard hesitated, torn yet again between his responsibility to George's health and the possibility that he could glean useful information about Raynor. Eventually, this time, the friend's instinct won through. The look of genuine concern on the sister's face saw to that.

'Yeah,' he said. 'Yeah, you're right. Of course you are.'

'I'm glad we agree. Would you like me to move George into a side room on his own? We've got one coming available in the morning — an old chap going out.'

'With a bit of luck, that will be George soon.'

'I do hope not, Inspector. This old chap will be going out in a box. Dead by morning, I reckon. His family filled in the breakfast menu for him but I couldn't help feeling they

151

were being rather optimistic. He's not going to be in the mood for Weetabix, if you ask me.'

'Ah.'

There was silence for a moment or two.

'I'm sure he will be OK on the ward. He likes the company,' said Blizzard eventually. 'How is he today?'

'He rather proves my point about a fragile recovery, I am afraid,' said the sister. 'After Morris left, George leaned over — we think he was trying to get his notebook out of the cupboard — and fell out of bed. Banged his knee.'

'Is it serious?'

'I don't think so, but these days you have to send them for an x-ray for the least little thing. Our beloved administrator is paranoid that we'll be sued.' She glanced at the clock on the wall and stood up. 'Now, I really have to go, gentlemen, there's always something to do around here and we've got a new admission due any minute.'

She gave them a sly look.

'Chap called Capone,' she said.

The detectives chuckled at the joke and followed her out into the ward.

'Thank you for your frankness,' said Blizzard, shaking her hand as they paused at the nurses' station. 'It really is most appreciated.'

'Anything that helps keep Morris Raynor and his cronies away from my ward is only to be welcomed, Inspector.'

'Do you mind if I just put this on George's bedside table before we go?' asked Blizzard, producing a bar of chocolate from his jacket pocket. 'It's his favourite.'

'Go on then,' she said. 'But be quick about it.'

Blizzard walked into the side room and over to George's bed. As he passed Harry Josephs, he noticed that the old man was lying with his eyes closed, his lips moving constantly. Something about him made Blizzard edge closer to the bed, keen to catch his words.

'It's wrong,' murmured the old man. 'It's wrong, it's wrong, it's wrong.'

'What's wrong, Harry?' said Blizzard quietly.

Josephs sat bolt upright and his eyes snapped open, startling the inspector, who recoiled slightly. They seemed to stare right through him.

'It's wrong,' said the old man. 'Just wrong.'

He sunk back onto the bed, closed his eyes and his lips stopped moving.

'What's wrong?' repeated Blizzard.

'Drugs,' said a voice behind the inspector. 'Drugs is wrong, although I'm not quite sure why what he's saying should be any of your business.'

Blizzard turned to see a middle-aged, grey-haired man walking towards the bed with a stern expression on his face.

'I'm sorry,' said the inspector, not quite sure why he was sounding so defensive again; it had been happening a lot lately. 'I didn't mean to eavesdrop on what he was saying.'

'Yes, you did. You're that detective. Seen your picture in the paper.'

'And you are?' Something about the man irritated Blizzard.

'Brian Harman.' He held out a hand. 'I work for hospital radio.'

'Haven't seen you here before,' said the inspector, reluctantly shaking the hand and finding the grip strong.

'Must have missed each other. I understand you come in here quite often.'

'Visiting an old friend.' Blizzard gestured to the empty bed by the window.

'Nice old stick is George.' Harman's expression softened and he winked at the inspector. 'For a poliss.'

Blizzard smiled slightly; the joke had broken the tension between the two men.

'Hang on,' he said suddenly as the thought struck him. 'How come you know about my visits?'

'Hospitals, Inspector, there are no secrets in hospitals.'

'Clearly not,' said Blizzard. 'And how come you know what he has been saying about drugs? Don't tell me he elaborated on his philosophy about narcotics while you were asking him which Tom Jones song he wanted playing?'

Harman did not seem offended by the comment.

'He has been saying it all afternoon,' he said. 'Ironic, really. Him being a villain.'

'How come you know he's a villain?'

'I know him of old, Inspector. Used to live on the east side.' Harman walked over to another of the beds and beamed at the elderly occupant. 'Leonard, you're awake at last. Thought you'd like to know I've managed to track down some Sondheim for you. It's a bit crackly but I should think it will play all right.'

The inspector placed the chocolate on George Moore's bedside table and walked back into the corridor.

15

As darkness fell over the scrapyard on the city's east side, Morrie Raynor sat in the back office, the small heater failing to dispel the deepening chill, and stared expectantly at the four men sitting in front of him. None of them returned the gaze.

'He's still letting his mouth go,' said Raynor. 'I thought this was supposed to be sorted.'

'Geoff was going to sort it,' said one of the men.

'Well, we all know what happened to him.' Raynor gave a thin smile.

The men shifted uncomfortably in their seats; no one dared ask what Morrie Raynor knew about the death of Geoff Bates. There were some things you did not say to Morrie Raynor. Des Fairley's death had taught them that many years previously.

'So,' continued Raynor, 'is someone going to sort this once and for all?'

All the men noticed that the temperature in the office seemed to grow even colder.

★ ★ ★

'This is ridiculous,' said Colley, tossing a student file onto the desk and looking across at Heather. He glanced up at the clock, which read 5.25 p.m. 'Maybe you were right. Maybe you did chase down all the angles last time.'

'Not that Blizzard's in the mood to believe it,' replied Morrison gloomily. 'Do you not think that he was a bit unfair to me earlier today?'

Colley held up both hands.

'Hey,' he said, 'you keep me out of this.'

The sergeant walked across to the pile of folders still waiting to be checked. He picked up the top one and found it empty.

'What's this then?' he said. 'The Invisible Man enrolled?'

'I'll see if any of the secretaries are still in,' said Morrison, walking over to the door into the main office.

She returned thirty seconds later with a middle-aged woman to whom Colley handed the file.

'This is empty,' he said.

'It shouldn't really be there,' said the secretary, glancing down at the name. She seemed uneasy. 'Her details will have been shredded.'

'Why so?'

'They always are with former students. Quite often folks forget to throw the folders out.' She gave the sergeant an anxious look.

'You won't tell the principal, will you? He's a real stickler for us getting the paperwork right and it's one of his big things.'

'It depends what her story is.'

'She left last term,' said the secretary. 'October-time, I think.'

'And why did she leave?' asked Colley.

'It's not really my place to say. She was a nice girl.'

'I am sure she was an absolute angel on earth,' replied Colley, letting his eyes stray to the larger pile of documents. 'But why did she leave Queen Mary's?'

The secretary gave him an unhappy look.

'I don't want to get her into any trouble,' she said. 'I don't think I should even be talking about former students.'

'Will you just tell us what happened?' The sergeant's voice had a hint of irritation.

The secretary looked round the room, as if hoping that salvation would appear. Returning her attention to the sergeant's stare, she sighed.

'The principal kicked her out because she was taking drugs,' she said. 'They were found in her locker.'

'Was she selling them to other students?' asked Colley.

The secretary looked away. Colley glanced at the DI. Bingo, his expression said. Bingo.

Alex Mather stood in the gathering late afternoon darkness behind a row of disused garages on the edge of a housing estate, rubbing his hands together and shuffling his feet as he tried to keep warm while he waited for his informant to arrive. As ever, the undercover officer had varied their meeting place to reduce the chance of detection and had declined the man's suggestion that they meet on the playing field again. Mather glanced at his watch. Hurriedly, he thrust it into his pocket as the luminous dial glowed in the darkness. Tensing as he heard footsteps, he looked up and saw the man appear by the furthest garage.

'Jesus, he's early,' murmured Mather, his instincts kicking in. 'He's never early.'

The man walked quickly over towards the detective. He looked more nervous than usual, his eyes darting to right and left as if he were frightened that they were being watched.

'Relax,' said Mather. 'I've checked it out. No one knows we are here.'

'This has to be the last time,' said the man, his voice betraying his anxiety. 'I can't meet you again.'

'Why not?' Mather tried to sound relaxed

but his heart was thumping and his palms felt clammy as he contemplated the possibility that he had been detected. Instinctively, his eyes scanned the area for anything untoward.

'It just has to be,' said the man evasively. 'Can't take no more risks.'

'What risks?'

'Look, there's some heavy stuff going off and I don't want to get mixed up in it.'

'Heavy like what?'

'If I tell you, you have to promise never to contact me again,' said the man.

Fighting the rising tide of panic, Alex Mather nodded.

'I promise,' he said.

The man looked at him suspiciously.

'I promise,' repeated Mather.

'You'll keep my name well out of this, yeah?'

'As ever.'

Ten minutes later, his story finished, the man looked at Mather, who handed him some banknotes.

'See why I'm worried?' said the informant, pocketing the cash.

'Yeah, but things have changed since — '

'Don't make the mistake of thinking he's yesterday's man.' The man turned to go. 'The last time, right?'

'The last time,' nodded Mather.

Once the man had gone, Alex Mather gave himself a few moments to calm down, waiting for his heart to cease its pounding. And as he stood in the darkness, one phrase reverberated round his head, time and time again. Don't make the mistake of thinking he's yesterday's man. Mather frowned. The detective had turned to go when he became aware of a scuffling sound and a muffled cry from beyond the row of garages. Mather started to run and within seconds emerged onto a small patch of wasteland, dimly lit by street lights from the nearby estate. Another cry drew his attention to two men standing on the far side of the wasteland. Mather could see that they were kicking something, again and again. He sprinted towards them, feet slipping on ice and stumbling over rusted tin cans and broken bottles. Hearing him approach, the men turned.

'What do you think you're doing?' one of them shouted.

Mather skidded to a halt and peered through the half-light at what was clearly the figure of a man lying on the floor. It did not move. Mather recognized the jacket.

'Who's that?' he asked, trying to stay calm.

'None of your fucking business!'

Mather wondered whether to reveal his true identity and arrest them but quickly discounted the idea; he had expended too much effort establishing his cover to blow it like this. Besides, he was not even sure he could take them on his own. Not even for an informant. The two men started to advance on him and one of them raised a hand. Mather cried out as he saw the glint of metal and hurled himself to one side as the knife flashed past his face. Regaining his balance, he snapped out a fist and caught the man in the ribs, hearing with grim satisfaction the grunt of pain as his attacker sank to his knees. A second snap of the fist from Mather sent the man crashing onto his side to writhe in pain, clutching his stomach.

Mather turned his attention to the second man but was too slow and felt the dull thud of pain as a fist slammed into his cheek, followed by another heavy blow to the face. Staggering backwards, Mather tried desperately to regain his senses as he saw, through blurred vision, the man advancing on him again. Mather shook his head and lashed out more in hope that judgement, his poorly aimed punch catching his assailant in the shoulder. The detective gave a smile of satisfaction as the man squealed in pain and staggered backwards, clutching the top of his arm. For a few moments, they faced each other.

'Go on,' said the detective, trying to remain calm, 'get out of here.'

The man hesitated but a step forward from the officer made his mind up and, after stopping to drag his groaning friend to his feet, the two of them staggered across the wasteland and out of view. Feeling his head begin to swim, Alex Mather gave a groan, his stomach heaved and he fell to the ground.

16

'You want to do what?' exclaimed the hospital administrator, a bearded man in his thirties, staring at the detectives in astonishment.

'We want to send in an undercover officer on Ward 46,' said Blizzard, keeping calm in the face of the man's fury.

'Why?' Michael Williams ignored Blizzard and looked at Ronald for support. 'Half of them think they're bloody Napoleon most of the time. What on earth would you want with any of them?'

'The chief inspector was, I think, going to explain that we believe that one of the patients could hold valuable information about an ongoing inquiry,' said the superintendent; like Blizzard he knew that such thoughts, when voiced away from the ward, sounded more than a little lame.

'Ongoing inquiry? What ongoing inquiry? Someone been nicking bedpans? It's rich even for your inspector's overactive imagination.'

He made the comment without looking at Blizzard. The three of them were sitting in the administrator's modern, and minimalist office, on the sixth floor of the General

Hospital and, in the tense silence that followed the outburst, Blizzard let his eyes range across the desk. He noted gloomily that it was empty apart from a monogrammed gold pen lying on a pristine blotter, and that there was nothing in the in-tray. Not a shred of paper. He wanted to ask the administrator how he managed to keep HR out of his office, but somehow it did not seem the time.

'Look, Michael,' said the superintendent, trying to strike a conciliatory tone, 'we really do have reason to believe that one of your patients can help us.'

'You've been listening to him too long,' said Williams, nodding at Blizzard. 'Him and his conspiracy theories. And presumably he's been listening to his friend George Moore. Well, he's barking as well.'

'That a medical term?' scowled Blizzard.

'But — ' began Ronald.

'But nothing, Arthur.' Williams stared hard at the superintendent. 'This is a backdoor way of spying on my pharmacy, isn't it?'

Ronald and Blizzard tried to look innocent.

'Because if it is . . . ' continued the administrator, wagging an accusatory finger at them.

'It's not,' said Blizzard, trying to remain calm. 'One of the patients in Ward 46 — a chap called Harry Josephs — is a former villain.'

'So?' snorted Williams. 'Aren't they allowed to get ill? Is there a law against that now?'

'That they get ill is exactly the point. You see, on this occasion we believe that Harry Josephs is about to unburden himself of some of his secrets about his criminal past.'

'Piffle, man! The only secret he is likely to reveal is whether he shagged Josephine or not!'

'It may be linked,' said Blizzard, trying hard to retain his composure, 'to an unsolved murder thirty years ago. If we have an officer working on Ward 46 undercover, they might pick up something useful.'

'The only thing they are likely to pick up is a nasty infection. I have never heard anything so ridiculous!' Spittle flew from the administrator's lips.

'Look,' said Ronald, trying again to defuse the tension in the room, 'we have received information — '

'From George Moore, no doubt,' snorted the administrator.

'It does not matter who it came from,' said Ronald. 'According to our informant, Harry Josephs has received visits from a number of well known members of the criminal fraternity since he came into your hospital.'

'So some of his friends visit him in hospital, so what?'

'We think he may be in danger,' said Blizzard.

'Danger?' The administrator's voice assumed a sarcastic tone. 'They going to get their 'shooters' out? This a 'blag'? They got to get their pyjama trousers on because they're nicked?'

Blizzard had heard enough.

'Listen you fucking halfwit,' he snapped, leaning forward in his chair, 'this is not some joke. One of the men who visited your ward was Morrie Raynor.'

'I do not think this warrants a descent into schoolyard abuse,' said Williams icily. 'And as for this Raynor fellow, I have never heard of the man. Who is he?'

'If you were a local man and not some southern pen-pusher parachuted in from London, you'd know. Morrie Raynor was one of the city's most notorious drug traffickers who — '

'So this is about my bloody pharmacy!' interrupted Williams, shooting a triumphant look at Ronald, who closed his eyes and wondered why he had allowed himself to become embroiled in the situation. 'I thought so! You've got those dead kids lying in my mortuary and you're desperate.'

'That's not fair,' began Ronald. 'But — '

'But nothing. It's a smokescreen and I've seen through it. And if you dare go to the

Press with any of this nonsense, I will take out an injunction against you. I've got fifteen million quid coming to this hospital and the last thing I want is bad publicity queering my pitch.' He stalked across the room and opened the door. 'Good day, gentlemen.'

Blizzard was about to speak but a sharp look from Ronald silenced him and the two officers stood up and left the office in silence.

'Got a Plan C, by any chance?' asked the superintendent tersely, as they walked down the corridor. 'Because Plan B was an absolute shambles.'

'I might pop back in on George later this evening. See what else he can tell us.'

'Might I suggest that you don't? I reckon he has said enough for one day, don't you?' Ronald stopped walking. 'Look, John, I hate to say it but your desire to get Raynor is clouding your judgement. I should never have let you talk me into this.'

Blizzard decided not to remonstrate with his friend and followed him quietly along the corridor. Ronald stopped at the lifts and pressed the button.

'Aren't you going to take the stairs?' asked Blizzard.

'No.'

'But it's better for your health if — '

'What's better for my health is not listening

to your cockamamie ideas.'

The tone of voice suggested the discussion was at an end and Blizzard decided that now was not the time to argue.

'Right,' he said.

As the detectives got into the empty lift and it started its downward journey, Blizzard's mobile phone rang. He removed it from his jacket pocket and placed it to his ear.

'John Blizzard,' said a gravelly voice from the other end, 'I understand you want to make my life even more ball-aching than it currently is.'

'Max,' said the inspector, trying to sound cheerful as he noticed Ronald's suspicious expression. 'Long time no speak, how on earth are you?'

'Well, I was all right until you decided to fuck up my murder investigation. Otter and Fish 8-ish? Your shout.'

'Yeah, see you there, thanks for your help on this one, Max, really appreciate it,' said Blizzard, slipping the phone back into his pocket.

'He OK about us getting involved in his case?' asked Ronald as the lift reached the bottom and they emerged into the ground floor corridor. 'Because the last thing I want is Eastern kicking off as well.'

'Says it'll be no problem. Reckons he'd

appreciate the input. It's a difficult case, apparently. Needs every bit of help he can get his hands on.'

'And he said all that in ten seconds did he?'

'Sort of,' said Blizzard evasively. 'I'm going to grab a cuppa before I go to see Jan Hennessey. Fancy one?'

'No thanks,' said Ronald, glancing at his watch. 'I said I would be home in time for dinner. It's embroidery night.'

'Oh, you've taken that up, have you? Good for you. Everyone needs a hobby.'

'My wife has taken it up,' said Ronald tartly. 'And I have to stay in with the dog. It's not been well and she wants me to watch it in case it throws up on the new rug again. I told her we shouldn't have got white.'

'Dog or rug?'

Ronald ignored the comment and headed off down the corridor.

''Night, Arthur,' said Blizzard.

Ronald waved a hand and lumbered round the corner and out of sight. Blizzard gave a chuckle and headed for the canteen. As he turned into the corridor leading to the café, he noticed a door which said 'Security'. The door opened and a dubious Blizzard surveyed the clean-shaven man who emerged from the office. A young man with short brown hair and the remnants of acne on his face, he was wearing a dark-blue security guard's outfit. To Blizzard, he looked as if he should still be at school.

'Jesus,' he murmured. 'Must be getting old.'

The young man noticed the inspector looking at him and walked over.

'Can I help you, mate?' he asked.

'Er, yes . . . ' said Blizzard, resisting the temptation to tell him they were not mates and instead peering at the badge on the young man's lapel. Unable to read it clearly, he had to move in very close, earning himself a strange look from the guard. *Keegan Rymes*, it said. The young man noticed the inspector's bemused expression when the detective straightened up.

'My Dad was a Liverpool fan,' explained the young man.

Blizzard still looked bemused.

'Kevin Keegan?' said the guard.

Blizzard still looked perplexed.

'Football,' said the young man.

'Ah, football,' said the inspector vaguely.

'Surprised you ain't heard of him, mind,' said the young man. 'Be your generation, I reckon. Seventies.'

Blizzard glowered at him but the young man seemed not to notice.

'Anyway,' said the young man, 'you look

like you needed some help? You lost? Need directing to the exit or something like that?'

'Not quite,' said Blizzard, reaching into his jacket pocket for his warrant card; the man looked a little more guarded now. 'I wanted a word about something that happened on Ward 46 last night. Your boss around?'

'He doesn't work nights. Leaves it to us younger ones.' The guard looked at his watch. 'Be in the pub, by now. Always has a couple on his way home.'

'This disturbance,' said Blizzard. 'You know anything about it?'

'Yeah. Me and Tel, he's one of the other lads, we got called up to sort it out. Some old blokes trying to get into to see a friend of theirs. Wouldn't be told that visiting time was over.'

'You call the police?'

'Na, they went good as gold when they saw our uniforms.' He gave Blizzard a proud look. 'I reckon they knew authority when they saw it.'

'They've never respected authority before, not sure they're going to start now.'

'Why you interested in them?'

'I'm not really.' Blizzard turned and started to walk towards the canteen; he had decided not to waste more time than he had to with the young man.

When the inspector walked into the canteen, still glowering, Amy was behind the counter, wiping down the work surfaces with a cloth. He brightened up when he saw her.

'Don't they ever give you a night off?' asked the inspector.

'That a proposition?' she said with a grin.

'Sorry, Amy, I'm a happily something-ed man. And according to your twelve-year-old security guard, an old man at that. In fact, I am so old I can even remember the seventies.'

'Which one said that?' she chuckled.

'He's named after a footballer.'

'Keegan?' She grinned. 'Don't mind about him. He's all right. In fact, we've been going out for three months now. Got together before Christmas. He bought me a lovely watch for a present. Real expensive it looked.'

She held up her wrist.

'It looks nice,' agreed Blizzard, resisting the temptation to tell her that she could do so much better than the security guard. He knew that it would only come out wrong. It always did when he tried to pay a woman a compliment. That's what Fee told him, anyway. Thought of Fee produced an unexpected stab of guilt. Did he look forward to his encounters with this attractive young girl because he liked flirting with her, the inspector asked himself?

'Penny for your thoughts?' asked Amy, noticing his silence.

'You'd need more than that, love,' said Blizzard.

'Not sure I've got it on my wages. Do you want something to eat?' she asked, gesturing to the serving counter. 'We've got plenty of lasagne left.'

'Er, no thanks,' said Blizzard. 'No offence, Amy, but I've never yet met anyone outside of Italy who can make lasagne properly.'

'You been to Italy then?'

'Er, yeah. Tuscany mainly.'

'I went to Italy once,' she said, her eyes assuming a wistful expression. 'Our parents took us to Florence. Beautiful it was.'

'Yeah, it is,' said Blizzard. The smell of cooking food reminded him that all he had had to eat had since breakfast was a couple of tired sandwiches. 'Any chance of those eggs again? They were excellent.'

'Since it's you. Tea as well, I assume?'

Blizzard nodded.

'Please,' he said.

'I saw your picture in the paper,' she said, turning and starting to make the drink. 'Front page news you were. I told Carol — she works here — I told her 'I know that bloke'. It's terrible what's happened to those teenagers, isn't it?'

174

'Yeah, it is. You know either of them?'

'Both of them.' She turned round, mug in hand. 'Bobby was at the same sixth form as me and Lorraine Hennessey. Nice lad. Bit quiet. Very good at art. Not the kind of person you'd expect to be involved in drugs. Only knew Charlotte to look at.'

'How come?'

'She had just started, the year below us.' She poured milk into the mug of tea and handed it to the inspector. 'I'll bring the eggs over when they're done.'

'Thanks,' said Blizzard. 'Out of interest, I assume we are talking about Queen Mary's?'

He tried not to sound too keen to hear the answer.

'You police officers,' she said with a light laugh, 'always asking questions.'

'Sorry,' said Blizzard with a rueful smile. 'Force of habit, I guess.'

'I'm sure it is. Well, since you ask, yes, Queen Mary's.'

'It's a good college from what I hear,' said Blizzard, taking a sip of tea. 'Very good reputation.'

He knew it was a bland comment, but a sudden instinct suggested that this was not the time to ask all the questions he wanted answering. Caution felt like the best approach.

'It was a bit stuck up for me,' she said,

lowering her voice and leaning forward, egg-box in hand. 'Between you and me, I got kicked out at the start of my second year. Before Christmas. That's why I work here.'

'Yeah?' Blizzard still tried not to appear too interested. 'What you do wrong? Been handing your homework in late?'

'I was found with cannabis one lunchtime. Apparently, it's not the done thing at Queen Mary's. The principal said I had let everyone down. Story of my life.' She gave a half smile. 'Hey, I don't know why I'm telling you this, you'll probably go and arrest me.'

'I will if you don't get those eggs on,' said Blizzard.

Realizing that even after all these weeks he did not know her surname, he tried sneaking a look at her name badge without appearing to be staring at her breasts; he knew how that would look. Having struggled to make out the letters clearly, he picked up his mug of tea, murmured his thanks and walked over to his usual table, realizing gloomily that it might be time to stop putting off his visit to the optician. He'd been experiencing increasing problems with reading things close up for several months; in addition to his innate dislike of paperwork, the headaches he increasingly experienced with close work was another reason he had been slow to complete the reports for Arthur Ronald. True to form, Blizzard had been deliberately ignoring the problems and had regretted confiding his difficulties to Fee, who had subjected him to constant nagging since she had found out.

Having sat down at the table, he pondered the eyesight issue for a few gloomy moments until the clatter of plates from the counter reminded him of his conversation with Amy. He surveyed her thoughtfully for a few moments, making sure that she still had her back turned. The inspector glanced round to check that the canteen was empty, took his mobile phone out of his pocket and dialled the number for the CID squad room.

'David,' he said in a low voice on hearing Colley at the other end. 'Do me a favour, will you? When you get chance, will you run a name through the database?'

'Who I am looking for?'

'A girl. I reckon she's about seventeen. Amy something couldn't quite make out the surname — Bebbington or Bedlington maybe. I didn't get a proper look at her name badge.'

'The light a bit funny, was it?'

'What?'

'Fee's right, you know, you really do have to make that optician's appointment. You'd look good in glasses — very distinguished, man of your age.'

Blizzard scowled but said nothing.

'This name, might it be Reddington?' asked Colley. 'Amy Reddington?'

'Could be.'

'I can tell you now that we haven't got anything on her.'

'How do you know that?'

'When we were going through the files at Queen Mary's, we discovered that she was kicked out at the end of last year on suspicion of taking drugs. Might even have been dealing. It was only cannabis but it sounded interesting.'

'Indeed it is,' murmured Blizzard, glancing back to the counter where Amy was still busy with the eggs. 'It gives us a link with all three victims.'

'Yeah, it does. Trouble is, her college file is empty and we're struggling to find out where she is now. How come you know about her?'

'She's making my tea.'

'Does Fee know?'

'Very funny.'

'I take it she's that girl at the hospital canteen you keep banging on about?' asked the sergeant.

'I don't keep banging on about her.' Blizzard realized that he sounded defensive again. 'Anyway, yeah, that's her. I do hope she's not mixed up in this. She's a bright kid.'

'Well, like it or not, she's the best lead we've got at the moment. You want me to come over?'

'No,' said the inspector, looking across to the counter as he heard the clink of cutlery. 'No, not yet. Listen, can you find out where the principal lives and see what he knows about her? Oh, and it might be worth getting a tail on her as well. Just in case she is our pusher. The last thing we want is her selling to any more kids. The canteen closes at nine thirty and I imagine she's on 'til then.'

'Yeah, I'll sort that. What are — ?'

'Got to go.'

Blizzard replaced the phone in his pocket as he noticed Amy bringing his meal over, giving him a cheerful smile when she placed it on the table. As she walked back to the counter, the inspector looked down at the plate; suddenly he did not feel hungry.

★ ★ ★

The luminous dial on Alex Mather's watch suggested that he had only been unconscious for a few seconds but it felt longer. Much longer. Long enough for someone to install a kettle drum band in his brain. Sitting on the icy ground, he tentatively felt his jaw, relieved to discover that it was not broken, then raised a hand to what was already a swelling on his cheek.

'Marvellous,' he groaned.

A thought struck him and he stood up, wincing at the pain caused by the rapid movement, and stumbled over to the figure lying on the ground. Looking down into the man's bloodstained and battered features, he feared at first that his informant was dead. A groan disavowed him of the notion and Mather crouched down over the man.

'Jamie,' he said, gently placing a hand on the man's shoulder. 'Hang on in there. I'll get help.'

The man did not reply and Mather could hear that his breathing was shallow and erratic. The detective stood up, reached into his pocket for his mobile phone and dialled 999.

'Ambulance,' he said. He wondered whether to reveal his real identity but when the ambulance operator asked for his name, all he said was: 'You don't need to know.'

Call made, he looked around to the nearby road and noticed that several front doors were open and that people were already heading in his direction. Alex Mather turned and disappeared into the darkness of the night.

★ ★ ★

Morrie Raynor sat in the back room at The Mitre and surveyed the two bruised and battered man standing front of him.

'So,' he said, 'do you have some good news for me?'

'Yeah,' nodded one of the men. 'We gave him a right good kicking.'

'It looks like he put up a fight. I did not have him down as the type.'

'Na, that was some bloke who tried to help him.'

'What bloke?' asked Raynor sharply.

'Some bloke who was passing by.' The man gave a crooked grin. 'Tried it on but we sorted him as well.'

'So who was he?' asked Raynor. 'This knight in shining armour?'

'Dunno,' shrugged one of the men. 'Just some bloke.'

'Had either of you meatheads considered the possibility that it might have been the under-cover police officer he's been talking to?' said Raynor, lips thin. 'And that you let him get away?'

The men looked at him in horror.

'Just get out,' rasped Raynor. 'Just get out of my sight.'

When the men had gone, Raynor produced a mobile phone from his pocket.

'Good job I arranged a bit of insurance,' he murmured.

Raynor dialled a number.

'You here yet?' he asked.

'Yeah,' said a voice on the other end, 'and it's fucking freezing.'

★ ★ ★

Blizzard had just finished his meal and was standing up to go when Brian Harman walked into the hospital canteen, saw the inspector and walked over to the table.

'Mind if I join you?' he said.

'Sure,' said Blizzard, resisting the temptation to tell him to go away.

'Fill up?' asked Harman, gesturing to the inspector's mug.

'Er, yeah — thanks.'

Several minutes later, the two men were sitting down together.

'I think we get off on the wrong foot,' said Harman after taking a sip of tea. 'Up there on the ward.'

'It happens with most people. Something to do with the job, I suppose. And I *was* eavesdropping on a seriously ill old man.'

'Nevertheless, I apologize for my somewhat brusque attitude.'

'No apology needed,' said Blizzard. It was clear that Harman had something to say but the inspector resolved to let him play the situation his own way. He opted for a bland question instead. 'How long have you been doing hospital radio then?'

'It'll be ten years in March. Took it up after I retired. My wife said I needed something to get me out of the house. I suspect it was her who needed it actually.'

'Probably,' said Blizzard.

Harman gave him a look.

'Sorry,' said Blizzard, 'that came out wrong.'

'I know what you meant. You married?'

'Er, no,' said Blizzard.

'My wife's dead now.'

'I'm sorry,' said Blizzard.

'And my daughter died last year. I'm all alone.'

'Ah.'

There was silence for a few moments.

'You and I have met before, you know,' said Harman. 'I mean, before this afternoon.'

'We have?'

'Like I said, I used to live on the east side. That's where I remember you from.' Harman chuckled. 'Don't suppose you remember me, mind. You were a young uniformed officer in those days — I was on my way home from work and you stopped me for riding my bike with no lights.'

Blizzard stared at him. 'I did that?' he said.

'Yeah. Like I said, you were only a young

'un. Real keen, you were. Gave me a right good lecture about road traffic law. Even cited the appropriate section.'

'Didn't realize I was that officious,' said Blizzard with a rueful smile.

'Wouldn't mind, but you missed the fact that I was three sheets to the wind.' Harman laughed out loud; the noise seemed to reverberate around the canteen, making Amy look over in their direction. He clapped a hand to his mouth. 'Sorry.'

'It's all right.' Blizzard looked at him. 'Look, what's this about, Mr Harman?'

'Ah, the detective's instinct, Mr Blizzard. I confess I had an ulterior motive for coming down here. I know you come here for a cup of tea after your visits.'

'How come?' asked Blizzard suspiciously.

'Hospitals have few secrets, Chief Inspector.'

'Clearly,' murmured Blizzard. 'When we were up on the ward, you seemed to suggest that you knew Harry Josephs?'

'From the old days,' nodded Harman. 'That's why I wanted to talk to you. See, when I was passing his bed earlier today — your friend George was asleep so he did not hear it. Oh, don't look so horrified, Inspector, everyone knows what he's been up to with that notebook — Harry kept saying that it was wrong. Drugs. Only this time he clearly thought he was talking to Morrie Raynor. And everyone knows how close they were.'

Blizzard looked at him keenly.

'OK,' he said, 'you've well and truly got my attention.'

'Good, because if you ask me, Raynor has got back into drugs and he asked Harry for his advice. He's always valued what Harry had to say. Everyone knows that.'

'Why are you telling me all this, Brian?' asked Blizzard curiously. 'I mean, why so interested? Surely you're taking a big risk if Morrie finds out. He's not exactly the most forgiving of characters.'

Harman gave the inspector a sad look.

'I saw that Lorraine Hennessey girl the other day,' he said. 'I was up on that ward. Don't usually go there. I caught a glimpse of her through the open door.'

Harman seemed close to tears.

'Reminded me of my daughter,' he said quietly.

'What did she die of?'

'She was killed crossing the road,' said Harman softly. 'By a young driver pumped up with drugs. That's why I want to help you.'

Harman lowered his voice and glanced round to check that Amy was still behind the counter.

'I take it you have heard the rumours about the pharmacy here?' he said.

'Yes, but we've drawn a blank.'

'Well, perhaps this will help. See, when Harry thought he was having this conversation with Morrie Raynor, he mentioned the name Malky.'

'You know anything more about him?' asked Blizzard, eyes gleaming.

'That's all I heard.' Harman glanced at his watch, drained his mug and stood up. 'Sorry, didn't realize that was the time. I'm doing the evening show. Playing some Sondheim for that bloke on 46.'

'Well thank you for your help,' said Blizzard, finishing his own drink and also standing up. 'I'd better go as well. Don't want to be late.'

'It's always later than you think, eh, Inspector?' said Harman, shaking the inspector's hand.

'Yeah,' said Blizzard thoughtfully, as he followed him out of the canteen, 'yeah, I guess it is.'

When Harman had gone, the inspector glanced over to make sure that Amy was still busy and dialled a number.

'David,' he said. 'Got another name for you.'

17

'I saw the article,' said Jan Hennessey quietly, glancing at the newspaper lying on the table in the corner of the living room. 'It said it had happened again.'

She looked at Blizzard, who was sitting in one of the armchairs, then at Heather Morrison, who was sitting in the other. The drugs squad officer averted her gaze.

'Is it true?' said Jan. 'Is the newspaper right?'

'I am afraid it is,' said Blizzard.

'But how could that be, Inspector?' Her question was delivered with a mixture of bewilderment and sorrow. 'I mean, how could you let it happen again after what happened to Lorraine? Heather, you said that you would do everything in your power . . . '

Her voice tailed off, there was no need for her to finish her sentence, and Blizzard did not reply immediately — partly because he wanted to phrase his words carefully and partly because he simply did not know what to say. Sitting there in the oppressive silence, he suspected that the words did not exist. And that even if he could find them, they would not even come close to easing the pain felt by Lorraine Henessey's mother. Heather Morrison stared at her shoes.

'I mean,' said Jan, 'it's been a year now.'

'I know,' nodded Blizzard. 'I know, and we should have caught whoever sold your daughter those drugs by now. If it helps, I have taken personal responsibility for the inquiry.'

'I am sure Heather did her best.' The comment was delivered in a flat tone, not lost on either of the detectives.

'I am sure she did.' Blizzard glanced at Heather and tried to look reassuring, 'but we need to do more. We really do.'

Jan glanced over to the mantelpiece where, next to an expensive gold clock and several ornaments, there stood a picture of a smiling Lorraine Hennessey, the original of the one which now hung on the noticeboard in the CID squad room at Abbey Road alongside those of Bobby Leyton and Charlotte Grayson.

'I imagine you do,' she said quietly. 'Do you have any lines of inquiry?'

'We are concentrating on Queen Mary's College.'

'That's what you did last time.' Jan looked at Heather Morrison and the comment sounded accusing.

'We are wondering if we missed something,' said Blizzard. 'Can I ask, does the name Malky mean anything to you?'

'Malky?' Jan shook her head. 'Sorry.'

Blizzard hesitated. Few decisions had seemed as difficult as the one he took now.

'Listen,' he said, 'please do not read too much into this, Jan, but does the name Amy Reddington mean anything to you?'

'Should it?'

'I am not sure.' Blizzard tried to select his words carefully. 'It's just that her name has cropped up a couple of times. If nothing else, I need to eliminate her from our inquiries.'

'My daughter mentioned her once or twice,' nodded Jan. 'They were not close friends, though.'

'Did you know that she was kicked out of the college for dealing drugs?'

'No, I didn't. When did this happen?'

'October time.'

'Then how could I know?' said Jan with a sad smile.

An image of Lorraine Hennessey sleeping in her hospital bed flashed into Blizzard's mind.

'Indeed,' he murmured. 'How could you?'

'Do you think she sold the drugs to my daughter?' asked Jan. The question was loaded and heavy. 'Is she the one, Inspector?

189

Her and this Malky?'

'It's just a routine inquiry.'

'It doesn't sound routine.'

'The last thing I want is people jumping to conclusions, Mrs Hennessey. We've already got dozens of parents contacting us to see if their kids are safe. I really don't want to inflame things any further.'

'And yet you asked if my daughter knew her.' Jan Hennessey eyed him closely. 'You must have had a reason.'

'I hope that I haven't.' Desperate to change the subject, the inspector glanced out of the window into the darkness of the night. 'Does your husband know what's happened? I noticed that his car was not in the drive.'

'It never is. He's away on business again. He took it really badly. Lorraine was his little girl and when that phone call came in, everything changed. You never think . . . you just never think . . . '

'I understand,' said Blizzard.

'He never talks about it, you know. Well, not to me anyway.'

Blizzard noticed a change in her tone of voice.

'But he does talk to somebody?' he asked.

'I think,' said Jan Hennessey, her voice heavy, 'that you probably already know the answer to that one, Inspector. Don't you?'

Once back in the car, Blizzard phoned Colley.

'Anything on this Malky character?' asked the inspector.

'Not yet. How did it go with Jan Hennessey?'

'Not good. Listen, keep trying with Malky, will you?'

'Yeah, sure, where will you be?' asked Colley.

'Got to meet Mather.'

'Bloody hell, thought he was dead!'

'I'll pass on your kind comments.' Blizzard heard a low chuckle at the other end of the phone.

Blizzard pocketed the phone and started the car engine then glanced over at Heather Morrison, who had said nothing since leaving the house.

'All right?' he asked.

'I missed it, didn't I?' she said quietly.

'I have this awful feeling,' said Blizzard, guiding the car out of the cul-de-sac, 'that you did.'

* * *

'I really am not sure I can help you any further,' said the college principal, looking at the sergeant then nodding towards Fee. He

191

sounded irritated. 'I told your colleague everything I knew earlier on today. I really do not have anything to add.'

'Just a few more questions,' said Colley. 'Purely routine, you understand, Mr Morton.'

'Well make it quick, I'm off out to a pub quiz.'

Colley glanced up at the clock, which said half past seven. He and Fee Ellis were sitting in the principal's tidy living room, the shelves of which were packed with neatly arranged books and whose mantelpiece was lined with trophies, each one polished and gleaming. Colley looked closer; they were all for pub quizzes. The sergeant sighed.

'Come on then,' said Brian Morton, a bespectacled, balding man in his forties, 'what is it you want to know?'

'Some information about one of your students,' said the sergeant.

'One of the dead ones?'

'No.' Something about the way he had uttered the words irritated the sergeant. 'Not one of the dead ones.'

'I think that came out wrong,' said Morton, noticing the sergeant's expression. He tried to look more contrite. 'This has been very upsetting for all of us. I hope you can understand that. None of us has been thinking straight.'

'You're thinking straight enough to go to a pub quiz,' said the sergeant tartly.

Morton looked uncomfortable but did not reply.

'Let me level with you,' continued Colley. 'We are working on the theory that one of your students supplied the drugs.'

'And who might this student be?' The principal's voice was guarded now.

'Amy Reddington.'

'She is a former student,' said Morton quickly and looked suspiciously at the detectives. 'How do you know about her anyway?'

'We were going through the files at your office,' said the sergeant. 'Came across her name.'

'But her details had been expunged, surely.'

There was something about the way he said the word 'expunged' that irritated the sergeant even further and he glanced at Fee Ellis, who raised an eyebrow. Neither of them found themselves enamoured to the college principal, not helped by the way he kept glancing at the clock.

'Expunged or not, her folder was still there,' said Colley, 'but it was empty. We would like to know what it contained.'

'Is she a suspect?'

'We have to explore every avenue open to us.'

'Which does not answer my question, Sergeant. Is she responsible for selling drugs to these poor young people?'

'I do not want to say anything more at the moment. Why did she leave?'

'It was nothing to do with the dead kids,' said Morton quickly. 'I can assure you of that.'

'That's being somewhat economical with the truth,' said Ellis. 'She *was* taking drugs, after all, and possibly dealing them to other students as well. You can see why that makes her of interest to us, can you not, Mr Morton?'

'I can assure you that we dealt with the situation effectively and quickly. We acted in a highly responsible manner at all times. Highly responsible. Yes, highly responsible.' Morton hesitated and leaned forward in the armchair. 'Look, I am not one to condone the use of illegal stimulants, and I would hate this comment to become common knowledge, but it was only cannabis we found her with. If it had been something harder like heroin, it might have been different, but cannabis? Surely all of us when we were younger have experimented with a bit of weed. I know I . . .'

His voice tailed off as he saw the detectives' stern expressions.

'There's plenty of evidence to suggest that some people gravitate to harder drugs having started on cannabis,' said Colley, his voice hard-edged. 'In fact, two years ago I dealt with the case of a twenty-four-year-old boy who hurled himself in front of a train while on LSD. Do you know what his first drug was, Mr Morton? Cannabis, that's what it was.'

'Ah, yes, yes, of course.' Morton seemed flustered by the sergeant's passionate response. 'Yes, you are absolutely right. Of course you are. That is why we dealt with this unfortunate situation so swiftly. Swiftly and responsibly. Yes, swiftly and responsibly.'

'So what happened?' asked the sergeant. 'How come you knew what Amy Reddington was doing?'

'We found some of the drug in her locker during a routine search.'

'Do you always search students' lockers?' asked Ellis, looking surprised.

'There had been rumours that some of the students had been taking drugs on campus. One of my staff had seen several of them round the back of the building a couple of days before. At first, he thought they were just smoking but when he got closer, he detected the aroma of cannabis.'

'How did he know what it smelled like?'

'Some questions you don't ask,' said the

principal with the slightest of smiles. 'Anyway, the students denied it, but when he brought the matter to my attention, of course I had no alternative but to take action.'

'By searching lockers?'

'We searched every locker, yes.'

'Why not just search the ones belonging to the students in question?' said Ellis.

'We would not have found the drugs belonging to Amy Reddington had we not done so, Constable.' He sounded proud. 'She was not one of the three students apprehended by my colleague, you see. Besides, I felt we had no option but to do a search of every locker.'

'How so?' asked Ellis.

'What you maybe fail to appreciate, Constable, is that Queen Mary's is a very special college and one that has a reputation built up over many years. Our students are the cream of the city's young people and their parents occupy very influential places in society. They expect us to ensure that the most exacting of standards are upheld and that includes a hard line on drug use. That is why I would appreciate it if you did not tell anyone else about my little slip when I was talking about cannabis. Of course, it's absolutely right that we take action in such circumstances. We do not want our college infected by undesirables.'

'And was Amy Reddington an *undesirable?*' Colley found himself bridling even further at the man's attitude. 'That why she was expunged from your college's history?'

'I am not sure I like the tone of the question, Sergeant. What you have to realize is that Amy Reddington was a somewhat headstrong young girl who was not averse to voicing her opinions in the most strident of language.'

'And that was what made her undesirable, was it?' asked Ellis. 'That she had a head on her shoulders?'

'No, of course not. Of course not.' Again the principal seemed flustered. 'We encourage our students to be open and challenging in their approach to the world but one has to be so careful these days. Standards, Constable. Standards in all things. I am afraid that Amy Reddington's behaviour was a cause of concern in that respect.'

'So *was* she dealing drugs?' asked Ellis.

'I cannot say for certain, but we were not prepared to take the risk.' Morton shook his head. 'Sad — a nice girl when you got to know her.'

'But headstrong,' said Ellis, staring at him.

'Yes.' Morton gave her a weak look. 'Headstrong.'

Ten minutes later, the detectives were walking back to the car, Ellis seething silently. Once they were in the sergeant's vehicle, she broke her silence.

'What a shit!' she exclaimed. 'What an utter sanctimonious shit.'

'Now, now,' said the sergeant, turning the key in the ignition, 'that's enough of that headstrong behaviour, my girl. You heard the man. Standards in all things.'

Fee noticed the impish look.

'Well, what do you expect me to say?' she said with a rueful smile. Then she frowned. 'What did you make of what he said about Amy Reddington? She our girl?'

'Doubt it. It's not as if she has made a secret of the fact that she was booted out for using drugs.' Colley glanced at her. 'A fact she let slip to Blizzard while making his tea, might I remind you. Sounds all rather cosy actually. Maybe you've got a bit of competition there, Fee my girl. After all, he's always had a thing for younger women has our Blizzard.'

'Just drive the car,' said Ellis, shooting him a withering look. 'And keep your trap shut while you're doing it.'

Colley grinned.

18

Before Blizzard left the hospital after his meal in the canteen, he went back to Ward 46, this time eschewing his healthy principles and taking the lift, feeling weary at the end of what felt like it had already been a long day.

'Now, now, Mr Blizzard,' said Maureen Cox as she let him through the doors, 'you know that visiting time does not start for another forty minutes.'

'What if I said it was official business?'

'I thought we agreed that you would not disturb George with this nonsense.'

'That's what I want to tell him.'

She looked at him suspiciously.

'Honest,' he said.

'Wait in the lounge then, I think it's empty. I'll bring him along.' Maureen gave him a look. 'And remember, I'll know if you go back on your word. Doubtless it'll be in his notebook.'

'Doubtless.'

Five minutes later, Blizzard was standing and staring out across the lights of the city centre, noting that the flecks of snow were starting to fall, when the lounge door opened and Sister Cox wheeled George Moore over to join him.

'Two minutes,' she cautioned. 'Then I'm kicking you out.'

'That's all I need,' said Blizzard. 'I don't really want to be here if Morrie Raynor turns up again.'

She nodded and left the room. George glanced up at the clock on the wall.

'You're very early,' he said eagerly. 'Something happened?'

'How's your leg?'

'Stuff my leg. What's happening?'

'Listen,' said Blizzard, dragging up a chair and drawing it close to the old man. 'I'm sorry about this, George, but there's no way we are sending anyone in undercover.'

'Why?' His disappointment was clear.

'Look, there's not an easy way to say this, George, but everyone thinks what you are saying is crazy. That it's the illness talking. Even I'm starting to have my doubts.'

'I'm not surprised,' said George knowingly. 'Folks have always been scared to go up against Morrie Raynor. He's still got plenty of friends, has Morrie.'

'It's nothing like that.'

'I tell you, John,' said George and shot out a bony hand and gripped the inspector by the wrist, 'Raynor is up to something and Harry

Josephs knows what it is.'

Blizzard wondered whether or not to take his friend into his confidence — and decided against it.

'Sorry, George,' he said, 'it's just — '

'Take me back, John.'

'What?'

'Take me back. I feel tired.'

George's flat tone suggested that the conversation was at an end and Blizzard sighed and took hold of the wheelchair handles. Ten minutes later, he was sitting in his car in the hospital car-park, dialling a number on a mobile phone as the snow whipped against the vehicle's windscreen.

'Ramsey,' said the detective inspector's voice at the other end.

'Chris,' said Blizzard, 'what's happening?'

'Reynolds got those test results back earlier than expected. Both Bobby Leyton and Charlotte Grayson had taken Valium and methadone laced with a strong alcohol. Vodka seems most likely.'

'Which confirms what we thought.'

'Makes it more likely that it's a kid pushing the stuff, though,' said Ramsey. 'Hardly the most sophisticated way to adulterate a drug.'

'Not sure you're right on that one, Chris,' said Blizzard, reaching to start the engine and switch on the heater and windscreen de-icer.

'The more I hear, the more I am convinced that the answer to this lies on the east side.'

'You not thinking that Morrie Raynor might be linked to this in any way, by any chance?'

'No. Yes. Not sure.'

'I think that's covered every possible answer, guv. Mind if I ask the question again?'

'No, forget it.' Blizzard sighed. 'Look, I don't want to go over old ground again, Chris, I really don't. I know everyone thinks I've gone off on one about Raynor.'

'I don't.'

'You don't?'

'You were right, guv, this inquiry foundered because we did not ask enough questions,' said Ramsey. 'So what if it turns out to be one of George Moore's wild goose chases? At least we asked.'

'Thank you.' Blizzard's response was heartfelt; it had been a lonely day. 'Thank you, Chris.'

'I'll see if we haven't missed something. Talk later.'

'Yeah,' said Blizzard, unable to conceal the smile. 'Yeah, we will.'

He was about to replace the phone in his coat pocket when it rang again. It was a short conversation, a matter of seconds, and having completed the call, he drove out of the hospital car park and towards the east side of Hafton. Having headed down the city centre ring road, which was a mass of bumper to bumper headlights in the early evening rush hour, the tower blocks of central Hafton disappeared and he passed into the eastern end of the city, rundown terraced streets to his left and, to his right, derelict industrial areas hugging the river.

As he drove, the inspector frowned more than once at the effect that the tough economic times were having on the city in which he had lived since his teenage years. Driving past familiar landmarks, a closed pub here, a boarded-up shop there, his mind went back to his days with Eastern, very early in his career. Formative times. Times when men like George Moore taught him so much of what he now knew. The east side had been a different place in those days. Alive. Vibrant. Yet to be hit by the recession that would strike it within a few short years, laying waste to a century and a half of industry.

Navigating along the main riverside road, past darkened terraces, Blizzard remembered how on every street corner would have stood thriving pubs, all lights, laughter and intrigue. Intrigue because with affluence came Morrie Raynor, whose presence seemed to over-shadow everything that happened on the east side. As a young officer learning his trade, Blizzard had not really dealt with Raynor. Raynor was the big league and Blizzard had found himself dealing with low level crime. Yet it was not possible for him to escape the name. He would hear it uttered in the canteen and in the squad room, would hear the stories about someone beaten up here, another threatened with a knife there, a pub landlord like Vic Cox forced to play ball in return for keeping his windows intact. The east side in those days was Morrie Raynor's world and every pub, every shop, every business, every home was touched by him in some way.

Blizzard had been a very different person in those days and, driving through the darkness now, it seemed a long time ago. He rarely had cause to visit the east side now and had not driven the road for the best part of six months. The last time, he recalled, was a trip with Fee to a bathroom showroom housed in a former Methodist church — something about shower fittings, he vaguely seemed to recall. He had not really taken much interest, just nodded in what he assumed to be the right places, grunted his assent when it seemed to be required and fished out his credit card when told what he had decided. Heading round a corner towards where the bathroom showroom stood, he saw without surprise that the business had closed and that the building had been boarded up. A sign, he thought, of Hafton in the nineties.

Shortly after he left the eastern edge of the city, and the houses began to peter out to be replaced by frozen fields hidden in the darkness, Blizzard turned right off the road to drive down a narrow gravel path, which wound its way across wasteland before ending in a deserted car-park overlooking the river. The snow had slackened off now and, parking the Granada, Blizzard stood on the foreshore for a few moments and stared out across the River Haft, turning up his coat collar against the sharp chill of the night as he listened to the gentle lapping of the waters. He found it a strangely reassuring sound. Always had.

The sound of approaching footsteps put an end to his brief reverie and the inspector turned to see a man emerge from the shadows, feet crunching on the pebbles. Even though he knew who it was, the inspector tensed until, as the man walked closer, he was able to confirm that it was Mather. The undercover officer looked older than when last they had met. Blizzard realized that the straggly beard was designed to make him look down-at-heel, but there was something in Mather's gait, and when he got nearer, a sense of darkness behind the eyes, that shocked the inspector. Then there was the swelling on his cheek and the dried blood on his chin.

'You look shit,' said Blizzard.

'Thanks for that,' said Mather, his gentle Scottish lilt thickened by a split lip. 'I feel better already.'

The undercover officer glanced across the wasteland and to the main road with the distant headlights of cars. Satisfied that no one else was present, he relaxed and shook Blizzard's hand. To the inspector, the grip felt clammy. Unhealthy.

'You can't keep this up for ever, you know,' said Blizzard. 'Got to come in sometime.'

'You sound like my gaffer.' As ever, Mather's voice was quiet and Blizzard had to strain to hear it above the lapping of the river. 'He's been saying it for months.'

'Maybe he's right. I mean, look at the state of you.'

'Yes, but, like I tell him, I'm finally getting somewhere.' Mather looked out across the river. 'That Russian vice ring we broke up earlier this year? The one with those eight kidnapped women? We wouldn't have got them but for me. Took me six months to get my informant to trust me enough to spill the beans.'

'But the cost, Alex,' said Blizzard, shaking his head, 'think of the cost.'

'You're going soft,' said Mather.

Blizzard knew that there was truth in the comment, that he would not have said, or even thought, such things before the birth of his god-daughter, that the arrival of baby Laura and his subsequent conversations with Fee about starting their own family, had changed the way he viewed the world. Fee said it had made him more human. Blizzard was not sure if it was a good thing or not.

The inspector looked again at Mather. His concern for one of his few true friends was genuine, fuelled because he knew the sacrifices that Alex Mather had made to feed his obsession with arresting the villains that many other officers regarded as untouchable. Blizzard had heard from the man's own lips the story of how his baby had been terrified when she saw his bearded face when he came home one night after being out of contact for the best part of a month. How the baby had not recognized him then and had feared him afterwards, how Mather's wife was convinced that the bearded monster was responsible for the child's recurring nightmares in the weeks that followed.

Blizzard had also heard Mather speak — but only once and then when his tongue was loosened by too much red wine — about the night he came home to find a letter propped up on the breakfast table and the house dark, silent and empty. That had been more than a year ago and Blizzard knew that Mather's wife had left no forwarding address, had made clear that she did not want him to come looking for them and had filed for divorce only through the medium of a lawyer under orders not to divulge their whereabouts and who zealously protected their secret. As far as Blizzard knew, and no one really knew much about Alex Mather's life, the detective had been as good as his word and had not tried to find them.

As he and Mather stood staring out across the river for a few silent seconds, the inspector knew why these were troubling thoughts. He knew that he had once been like Mather, putting his career in front of everything. That was why Blizzard's own marriage had collapsed many years previously, his wife hurling accusations of selfishness and uttering the old cliché that he was married to the job when she stormed out of his life at the end of that final shouting match. Blizzard had enjoyed the years that followed and he could see now the attraction of the path his friend had chosen; a life without emotional attachments, and talk of shower fittings and curtain rails, was a much less complicated existence. For John Blizzard, it was a disturbing thought.

'Peaceful, isn't it?' said Mather, staring out across the river.

'Yeah. Yeah, it is.'

'Sometimes, I get this overwhelming urge to walk out into the water and let myself sink to the bottom.'

'What kind of talk is that?'

'You're right, John.' Mather turned heavy eyes on his old friend. 'Maybe it is time to pull out. I've been toying with the idea for a few weeks.'

He raised a hand to his injured face.

'Can't keep doing this kind of thing.'

'There's got to be a limit,' nodded Blizzard. 'Every man has one.'

'Yeah, I know, but I'm just not sure I can go back to a normal life. You want to know my real fear? Even more than being rumbled?'

'Go on.'

'Sitting in an office going through traffic forms. I mean, can you really see me doing that, John?'

Blizzard's thoughts strayed to his overflowing in-tray and shook his head.

'No,' he said. 'No, I can't. You really thinking of pulling out?'

'Not sure, John, I really am not sure. Carol's solicitor has made it clear that she does not want to see me again. She reckons the little 'un is better off without me in her life.' His voice trembled slightly. 'What is there to go back to?'

'Maybe she'll change her mind if you go back to more sensible hours,' said Blizzard, placing a reassuring hand on his friend's shoulder.

'Can't see it, John.' Mather sighed.

'You'll feel better after a shave,' said Blizzard, removing his hand from the shoulder.

The inspector's comment lightened the atmosphere and Mather gave a light laugh.

'Yeah,' he said, 'yeah, I guess I will.'

'Is that why you invited me down here?' asked Blizzard. 'Help you make your mind up?'

'No. It's about your dead kids again. Got anyone in the frame for it yet?'

'Few half leads. There's a girl who got kicked herself out of college for dealing a bit of weed, but not sure about her yet. She's not exactly trying to keep it a deep, dark secret. And we've been given a name — Malky. Mean anything to you?'

'Sorry. However, I may have something which could help.' He touched his swollen face. 'I think that's why my informant was turned over.'

'You think one of your east-side villains supplied the gear?' asked Blizzard. He had resolved not to mention his suspicions about Raynor unless Mather did. The inspector realized that he needed a clear head as the inquiry unfolded, one without George Moore's conspiracy theories.

Mather was about to reply when he looked round quickly at the sound of footsteps on the pebbles. Blizzard followed his gaze and saw a man and a dog making their way along the shore.

'Time to get out of here,' said Mather.

'Relax. Looks innocent enough.'

'In my world, there's no such thing as innocent.'

Neither officer spoke as dog and owner approached, the man tensing for a few moments as he flashed his torch in their direction, dazzling the officers for a few moments.

'Evening,' said Blizzard calmly.

The man gave them a strange look then he and his dog ambled off up the path and out across the wasteland.

'Probably thinks we're on a gay tryst,' said Blizzard with a laugh. 'But don't get your hopes up, I never do it on the first date.'

'The way my love life's going, you may be

my best option. Mind, your lass is more attractive than me. No crap beard for a start.'

'Get off — the last thing she wants is some vagrant pestering her.'

Both men chuckled as they watched the dog owner's light fade into the darkness until finally it was extinguished.

'Sorry about panicking,' said Mather. 'This job makes you paranoid. Look, there is one person you might look at for your drug dealer. That's why I wanted to see you.'

'Got a name?' Blizzard felt strangely tense.

'You didn't get this from me — the last thing I want to do is get involved in the politics — but I've been hearing things about your old friend Morrie Raynor.'

'What things?' There was a gleam in Blizzard's eyes.

'That he may have grown tired of retirement but that his old dealers won't supply him. Say he's soiled goods since he went inside. The word is that he's been looking at prescription drugs instead. Got plans to set up a network, apparently, but he's terrified that he'll go inside again if he gets caught. Word is he's doing everything possible to keep things quiet.'

'George Moore reckons some of his thugs are trying to silence Harry Josephs. They're in the same ward at the General.'

'It's possible, I guess,' nodded Mather. 'I did hear that Raynor still sees Harry. He always trusted Harry's judgement. Maybe Harry does know something.'

'Is there a link with the murder of Geoff Bates, do you think?'

'Not sure. Randall says not.'

'I'm off to see Max now. I'll ask him.'

'Yes, well, be warned, he's pretty spiky about you getting involved. Thinks you're sticking your oar into Eastern's business.' Mather turned to go. 'Come on, let's move. Already been here too long.'

As they made their way towards the inspector's car, Blizzard looked round for Mather's vehicle.

'Don't have one,' explained the undercover detective.

'You want a lift then?'

'Better not.'

The two men shook hands.

'Be careful, yeah?' said Mather. 'Remember what I told you about Raynor.'

'And you, eh? You be careful as well.'

Mather lifted a hand to his face.

'Sure,' he said with a wry smile. 'After all, what could possibly go wrong?'

Blizzard stood by his vehicle, watching Mather lope across the car-park.

'Hey,' called the inspector softly.

Mather turned round.

'You know where I am if you need me,' said Blizzard.

Mather lifted a hand in acknowledgement and disappeared into the darkness. Blizzard turned and stared back over the dark waters of the Haft and the showreel started to play again.

★ ★ ★

Morrie Raynor sat in the half-light of the scrapyard office, smoking a cigarette and surveying the grey-haired man standing before him.

'You sure you want him dead?' asked the man.

'Yeah,' said Raynor, blowing a puff of smoke. 'You'll have to wait until he leaves the hospital. Too much going on there at the moment with the cops sniffing around.'

'I'll find a way.'

'Yeah, well, do it properly,' said Raynor. 'Don't want no cock-ups.'

'Nor me, Morrie. I've taken a big risk coming back as it is. Where's the money?'

Raynor reached into his desk and produced a brown envelope.

'Half now, half when it's done,' he said, handing it over.

The man did not reply but turned and left the room. Morrie Raynor returned to his cigarette.

★ ★ ★

It was shortly after eight and the last of the evening visitors had left when the security guard Keegan Rymes walked into Ward 46 and up the corridor to the nurses' station, where Maureen Cox was catching up on some paperwork.

'Any of our friends come back?' asked Rymes.

'No one,' she said, not looking up from the document she was filling in. 'You must have scared them off.'

'I told Blizzard that but he didn't seem convinced. I don't think he likes me.'

'You saw Blizzard, did you?' she said, looking up and surveying him intently. 'Pray, what did he want?'

'He was on about Harry. Asking questions about his visitors and the like.'

'And what did you say, Keegan?' asked Maureen, eying him keenly. 'What did you tell the good inspector?'

'Didn't say nowt.'

'Good boy,' said Maureen, returning to the document. 'Good boy.'

19

The hitman edged his vehicle into the hospital car-park, cut the engine and settled down in the darkness. Anxious not to attract attention to himself, he decided to keep the engine off so he shivered more than once as the temperature dipped sharply in the car. Having flown into the UK from his home in Spain, travelling as always under an assumed name and on a false passport, he felt acutely the contrast between the Mediterranean warmth and the icy chill of Hafton. It reminded him of the reason he had left Britain all those years ago. That and the need to escape some inconvenient questions from the police. With a deep sigh, he sank back into his seat, cap tipped forward over his head, and waited for his man.

★ ★ ★

After the departure of Alex Mather, Blizzard guided his car across the wasteland and back on to the main road, following it further east as it hugged the banks of the Haft, passing through several small villages until he arrived at his rendezvous point in the river-bank community of Heslington. Blizzard pulled up outside the welcoming glow of a pleasant mock Tudor pub in the centre of the village. Getting out, he once again stared out across the river, noting how different it was here, somehow softer, more relaxed than the harsher, darker waters of Hafton's industrial lands that he had left behind.

He could have stood there for much longer despite the chill of the night, but after a couple of minutes, he turned and headed into the lounge of the pub, which was virtually deserted apart from a young couple in a window seat, eyes only for each other, too engrossed in themselves to notice his arrival, and sitting at a table by the fire a man in his early fifties, hair almost grey, thinning and cut short, his face chiselled and pock-marked, the eyes deep and dark. He was dressed in an ill-fitting dark navy suit with no tie. He looked like the kind of man who did not even own a tie. This was Detective Inspector Max Randall. For Blizzard and Randall, it had always been a good relationship whenever they had worked together, two old-school detectives struggling to survive as time passed them by and appreciating each other's qualities all the more for it.

Noticing the approaching inspector, Randall

downed the remnants of his pint and waggled his glass in Blizzard's directions.

'Smith's,' he said.

Blizzard nodded but said nothing. Like everyone else, he had heard the rumours that Randall's heavy drinking was now spiralling out of control and that the man was, to all intents and purposes, an alcoholic. Blizzard went to the bar and ordered two pints of bitter.

'That for Max?' asked the barman.

'Er, yeah.'

'He'll want a whisky in it,' said the man and reached for the bottle.

Having taken the drinks over to the table, Blizzard sat down and slipped off his jacket, appreciating the warmth of the open fire after the cold of the night.

'Cheers,' said Randall and the two men clinked glasses. 'You OK?'

'Yeah, not bad. You?'

'Wish I'd never accepted that damned promotion. Why didn't you tell me that DIs had to do so much shit?'

'I think some of them quite like it,' he said.

'Your bloke certainly does, from what I hear.'

'He does indeed,' said Blizzard, thinking of Ramsey and his love of paperwork and systems. He took a sip of beer. 'Bye, that's a nice drop, Max. You a regular here?'

Randall gave a slight smile.

'What do you think?' he said. 'Anyway, enough small talk. Haven't you got enough to do without meddling in my affairs?'

Although spoken in jocular fashion, there was an edge to the words.

'Long story,' said Blizzard, taking another sip of ale. 'Suffice to say that I've got Harry Josephs in a ward at the General, being visited by the likes of Morrie Raynor and Geoff Bates. Geoff Bates a few hours before someone put a bullet in him.'

'OK, I'm interested,' said Randall, taking a gulp of beer and wiping the froth of his mouth with the back of his hand. 'How come you're involved in this?'

'It's all down to George Moore — he's in the next bed to Harry Josephs.'

'A veritable gathering of old rogues,' exclaimed Randall loudly.

The barman glanced in their direction and even the loving couple dragged their eyes away from each other.

'Not sure I would describe him as that,' frowned Blizzard.

'You and I can agree to differ on George Moore if you want, John, but if you ask me, the man always had an overactive imagination.'

'That's what Arthur said but, be that as it

may be, George reckons that Harry Josephs is ready to spill the beans on a whole host of crimes and I simply cannot ignore that — and neither can you, Max. Think of the clear-ups.' Blizzard gave him a sly look. 'And from what I read of your recent stats, you could do with some clear-ups.'

'Below the belt, John,' said Randall, 'below the belt.'

'Nevertheless.'

Randall thought for a few moments and took another gulp of beer. Blizzard could see from the gleam in his eyes that he was interested in what he was hearing.

'Harry certainly knows a lot,' said Randall eventually. 'I guess the problem is that George Moore always was one for conspiracy theories. And I heard that he was in the hospital with some kind of infection — old folks say all sorts of weird things when they're ill like that. My old mum thought she was Ava Gardner.'

'Look, I don't want to be seen to be meddling in your investigation . . . '

'But you're going to anyway.' Randall gave him a grudging look. 'OK, maybe I could do with a little extra help. The top brass are jumping up and down demanding to know why we haven't lifted anyone for Bates's murder.'

'I take it you've not got much to go on?'

'Not really. He had a new woman in his life but she's not been much use. The bullet that killed him comes from an old service revolver. That's quite interesting. We've lifted a few old-timers, see what they know.'

'Morrie Raynor?'

'That's twice you've mentioned him, John. I can see where this is going,' said Randall, draining his glass and standing up. 'Pint?'

'Half.'

Randall grimaced.

'Driving,' explained Blizzard.

'So am I.'

Blizzard said nothing — knew he should have, but didn't — and Randall went to get the drinks.

'Let me level with you,' said Randall, returning with the glasses and sitting down at the table. 'I'm loath to get involved in anything concerning Morrie Raynor. My gaffer is one of those with long memories when it comes to him. I know you've got a thing about Raynor, John, but he really is history, you know.'

'Alex Mather would disagree.'

'You've seen him?' said Randall uneasily.

'I have, and so have you, I think. See, from where I'm sitting, Maxie-boy, it sounds like Eastern are planning to lift Raynor yourselves and grab all the glory.' Blizzard gave a slight smile. 'Surely, that's just me being an old cynic, though. I mean, surely there's no way that an old friend like you would hold out on me?'

Max Randall gave a sigh.

'Remind me not to drink with detectives,' he said.

* * *

The hitman looked out over the deserted hospital car park then glanced at his watch. 11 p.m., it said.

'Come on,' he murmured. 'Don't want to be here all night.'

* * *

Darkness had long since fallen on Ward 46, the lights in the side rooms switched off and the doors onto the main corridor closed. In the room containing George Moore and Harry Josephs, all was silent except for the snoring of an old man in the corner and the occasional moan from another patient over by the window. From time to time, the door from the main corridor opened and Nurse Alison Ramage walked in and surveyed the room. With the clock ticking towards two, she came in to do her usual check. She walked to each bed, looking down at each patient and made an entry on their clipboards. When she reached the window, she paused and stared out over the city, the street lights partially obscured by the thickening snow that had been falling since shortly before eleven.

Nurse Ramage completed her perusal and turned to George Moore, who was asleep. Occasionally, he muttered something but Nurse Ramage could not make out what it was, nor did she try.

* * *

Just after eleven, Alex Mather's informant walked unsteadily out of the main entrance at Hafton General Hospital, followed by a nurse.

'Please, Mr Smith,' she said, reaching out to take hold of his coat, 'will you listen to me? You really are not fit to go home. You have suffered a serious assault and — '

Jamie turned bruised and battered features on her and shrugged away her hand.

'Just leave me alone,' he said, through swollen lips. 'I'll be all right.'

'The doctor says you should at least stay in overnight. The x-ray shows a broken rib and we want to do further checks on . . . '

Her voice tailed off as Jamie turned and walked. The nurse stood and watched him go, shaking her head.

'It's your funeral,' she murmured.

She watched him walk unsteadily across the car park and, as he vanished into the snow, it seemed to the nurse that she heard the starting of a car engine.

★ ★ ★

Shortly before midnight, John Blizzard finally got to bed. Having left his car outside the pub in Heslington, realizing he was over the limit and leaving Max Randall still drinking, the DCI had taken a taxi to Abbey Road to catch up with progress on the drugs investigation. Having arrived just before ten, he had talked to the investigating team for a few minutes then Fee gave him a lift back to his home in one of the villages to the west of Hafton. Home for several years had been a modern house on an estate. Blizzard did not like modern houses and had always fancied the idea of living in one of the Victorian houses near the city centre. However, that area's decline had seen most of them converted into bedsits and he did not relish the thought of living among tenants with a somewhat flimsy grasp on the concept of law and order.

On arriving at his house, the couple sat in the living room and shared a bottle of red wine while discussing the events of the day, eventually going to bed as the clock ticked on to towards twelve, Blizzard gloomily acknowledging that he had consumed too much. As he climbed the stairs, realizing, as he missed his step a couple of times, that he was drunk, the inspector wrestled with the unpalatable truth that he would suffer with one of his bad heads in the morning. As the DCI had grown older, he had struggled to handle the effects of his drinking and, walking into the bathroom to clean his teeth, it was a troubling thought, one of many that had assailed him at the end of what felt like it had been a very long day. As snow drove against the window and the wind shrieked, he wondered how Mather was.

When he walked into the bedroom, Fee was already in bed from where she looked up from her book to watch him hang up his suit in the wardrobe.

'You going to wear that again tomorrow?' she asked.

'Yeah, why not?' He turned to look at her.

'Because you've worn it for the past week. It needs dry cleaning. Why not wear the grey one instead? You haven't worn that one for ages.'

'I don't like the grey one. Makes me look fat.'

'I'm saying nothing,' said Fee and returned to her book.

Blizzard sighed, removed his suit, crumpled it up and dropped it onto the *chaise-longue*.

'God knows when I'll get to the dry cleaners,' he said, getting into his pyjamas. He looked down at her and gave a smile.

'What?' she said, looking up again from her reading.

'Bye, you're a bonny-looking woman, and I love you to bits.'

'You pissed?'

'What makes you say that?'

'Because you always love me when you're drunk.'

'It's not that. I mean, I am drunk, obviously I am, but I'm not saying it because of it. I was just paying you a compliment.'

'Go on then,' she said, placing her book face down on the bedspread, 'what made you decide that I was bonny?'

'No beard,' explained Blizzard.

'You do say the nicest things. It's what attracted me to you in the first place.'

The inspector laughed and climbed into bed.

'I take it,' said Fee, picking up her book again 'that you are angling to have your

226

wicked way with me? It's about the nearest thing you are likely to get to a chat-up line.'

'No,' he said, 'not particularly. It's just something Alex Mather said tonight.'

'You didn't say you'd seen him. What was it he said?'

'That we are all getting old. At least, I think that's what he was trying to tell me.' He gave her a peck on the cheek, rolled over and snapped out his bedside light. 'Night, pet.'

The inspector did not go to sleep immediately but, having turned the case over and over in his mind, he finally drifted into an uneasy slumber. Shortly before three, and halfway through a dream in which Blizzard was back at school and Amy Reddington was his teacher, the inspector's bedside telephone rang. Blearily, he reached out and picked up the receiver.

'This had better be good,' he grunted, glancing at the luminous hands on the clock. 'Do you know what time it is?'

'Visiting time,' said Colley's voice.

'What?' Blizzard sat up.

'Harry Josephs is dead.'

20

Blizzard, suddenly alert and sober, stood at the end of Harry Josephs' bed and grimly surveyed the old man's face, the features finally at peace, the lips still and silent, the eyes closed, the constant contortions of the body stilled. The inspector peeked through the curtain surrounding the bed and looked round at the rest of the ward. All the other old men seemed asleep. Blizzard looked last at George Moore.

'Maybe you were right,' he murmured.

Blizzard turned round as Graham Ross and Peter Reynolds entered the dimly lit room.

'See what you can find, eh?' he whispered, and walked past them and out into the corridor to be confronted by a group of concerned nurses.

The inspector saw Colley and Ellis standing in the entrance to the office behind the nurses' station.

'They say we can use here,' said the sergeant.

Blizzard nodded and walked into the office.

'Well,' he said bleakly, sitting down behind the desk, 'one thing's for certain. Harry

Josephs is as dead as the proverbial and he's taken all his secrets with him. Who called it in? Do we know?'

'One of the nurses,' said the sergeant. 'Did her usual check and noticed that Harry Josephs was not breathing. She's waiting outside if you want to ask her.'

Blizzard nodded and Fee went out into the corridor, returning a few moments later with a young woman.

'This is Jane Hodgson,' said the constable. 'The nurse who raised the alert.'

'And why did you do that?' asked Blizzard, eyeing her closely. 'Harry Josephs was a seriously ill old man, wasn't he? Surely they die all the time?'

'They do,' she nodded, 'but we knew that you had been interested in him. The sister suggested we call you.'

'Was that Sister Cox by any chance?'

'No, she had already gone.'

'Are you sure?'

'Why wouldn't I be?'

'Just asking,' said Blizzard. 'Are you sure she had gone?'

'Her shift ended at ten. She said she was going straight home.'

'I'm sure she did. Did you see anyone near Harry's bed before you found out that he was dead?'

'No one. Everyone was asleep.'

'Had he had any visitors during the evening?'

'Not as far as I know. Mind, I only come on at ten.'

'And the nursing staff?' asked Blizzard. 'Where were they when you discovered he was dead?'

'Catching up on paperwork, most of them. Or having a cup of tea. We usually have one about this time.'

'Are you sure you know where everyone was, Nurse Hodgson?' he said. 'I mean, really sure?'

'Yes, I'm sure.' She sounded irritated. 'And I don't like your insinuation. None of us killed the old man if that is what you are thinking.'

'Assuming anyone did,' said Blizzard, looking up as Peter Reynolds walked into the office. 'And here is the man who may be able to tell us. Well?'

'No, he's definitely not,' said the pathologist, sitting down on the sofa and smiling when Blizzard closed his eyes, as he did every time the pathologist made the joke. 'Although quite why this could not have waited until the morning, Blizzard, I don't know.'

'We wanted everything done and dusted before the day shift comes on. Have you been able to find anything out?'

'Well, it's not easy to do anything like a proper examination in the circumstances,' said Reynolds tetchily, 'what with most of the lights out and surrounded by sleeping patients. I'm not used to working with the living, Blizzard. Why can't we ship him down to the mortuary so I can have a proper look?'

'We will do when Ross has examined the scene. What did you conclude?'

'Well, if he *was* done away with, and I remain to be convinced, a working hypothesis might be that he was smothered with a pillow, I suppose. But there are no marks on his neck. Mind, it would not take much effort to send him back to his Maker. He was a scrawny old goat.'

The nurse made a little noise.

'Get her out of here,' said Blizzard to Fee, realizing that the words came out curtly. He tried to sound more sympathetic as the nurse started to cry. 'And thank you, Jane. Thank you for your help. Constable Ellis will take a full statement from you.'

With a sharp look at the inspector, Ellis took the distressed young girl out into the corridor, where she was comforted by a group of her colleagues.

'You really do have a remarkable bedside manner,' said Reynolds, looking at Blizzard. 'I had rather fondly hoped that you reserved your most acerbic comments for me, but it seems that anyone is fair game in your world.'

'Can we get on with the job in hand?' scowled Blizzard. 'Any idea when chummy died?'

'I don't think he's been dead for long. I'll know better after the post-mortem. I'll check for poison as well. In the meantime, it depends on how regularly the nursing staff checked on him.'

'Ah, I can answer that one a little more precisely,' said Colley, reaching out to the desk for a clipboard. 'According to this, he was checked every hour on the hour. The last check before the alarm was raised was just before two o'clock. So assuming the chart has been filled in correctly, that puts Sister Cox in the clear.'

'In theory,' said Blizzard.

'I can't understand why you are so interested in the good sister,' said Reynolds. 'She always struck me as an admirable woman. More prone to caring for her patients rather than bumping them off, I would have said.'

'I am sure you would, but of all the people on this ward, she is the one with most reason to see Harry Josephs dead.' The inspector glanced at Colley. 'Dark waters run there, David, you mark my word.'

'If you say so,' said Colley, but he did not sound convinced.

'I sense that the sergeant shares my misgivings,' said Reynolds, standing up. 'I just can't see Maureen Cox doing something like this. Salt of the earth, that woman.'

'Maybe you are right,' said Blizzard wearily, as Reynolds walked out of the office, standing aside to allow Ross into the room, immaculate in his grey suit despite the hour. 'Versace, it would really help if you found the murderer hiding under the bed clutching a pillow. Make life a hell of a lot simpler.'

'Sorry, guv. In fact, I found remarkably little. Look, are we sure this really is a murder? There's absolutely nothing to suggest that he was attacked. Is it possible that what with all the police interest in the old fellow, the nurses just over-reacted?'

'Who knows?' shrugged Blizzard. 'Hey, is George Moore awake yet by any chance?'

'He's dead to the world, guv.' Ross glanced at Colley and grinned. 'As it were.'

'You two should go on the sodding stage,' sighed the inspector. 'You really should.'

★ ★ ★

After discharging himself from the hospital, Jamie made the short walk into the city centre and caught the last bus over to the east side. The vehicle was virtually empty and during the twenty-five-minute journey, the informant stared silently out into the darkness of the night, occasionally reaching up to feel his bruised face. He did not notice the car driving slowly behind the vehicle, the swirling snow illuminated in its headlights. Alighting outside a row of shops at the heart of the housing centre, he glanced nervously right and left then headed through the alleyway which led to the square in which he lived. At first, Jamie did not see the man when he stepped out from the shadows ahead of him. It was only when he moved into the arc of light thrown by a nearby street lamp that he saw him.

'I told you to keep away,' he said, pointing to his battered face. 'Look what talking to you did to me.'

'Sorry,' said Mather, 'just one more question.'

'One,' hissed the informant, glancing along the alley to make sure that no one had seen them. 'One and that really is it. Do you understand?'

Five minutes later, and hugging the shadows, Alex Mather made his way off the housing estate. He did not see the man step out of the alleyway and screw the silencer onto his gun.

'So what do you want to do about Maureen Cox?' asked Colley, as he and Blizzard sat in the small office, sipping cups of tea made by one of the nurses. 'Do we bring her in? She's the only one with a reason to murder Harry Josephs. She could easily have come back after her shift ended. Maybe one of the nurses is covering for her.'

'A conspiracy theory of which George Moore would be proud, Sergeant. No, we have to go slowly on this one until we know exactly what has happened. You've seen how fast rumours spread round this place. Got to keep things low key.'

He was about to open the office door when a furious hospital administrator barged into the room.

'What was that about low key?' murmured the sergeant, earning a pained look from the inspector for his trouble.

'What is the meaning of this?' hissed Michael Williams, glaring at Blizzard. 'Two bloody coppers just demanded my identity before they let me in.'

'You've got a suspicious death,' said Blizzard. 'Our friend Harry Josephs.'

'This isn't Emergency Ward Ten,' snapped Williams. 'Old men get ill, old men die, end of story. It comes with the territory. I've got a good mind to get security to throw you out of this — '

'Why don't you come down off your high horse and start to act sensibly?' snapped Blizzard. 'Like it or not, something strange has been happening in this ward and now the patient at the centre of it is dead. It may well be perfectly natural, but until we know for sure, I would suggest that we find a way to work together. It was your nurse who called us, remember.'

William considered the comment and nodded, his bluster dissipating.

'OK,' he said, sitting down on the sofa. 'OK, Blizzard, have it your way, but I would appreciate it if we can keep this out of the Press until the end of tomorrow.'

'Why?'

'That's when they make the decision about the funding. I really do need to keep a lid on things until then.'

'Not sure we can do that,' said Blizzard. 'You seem to have a very effective grapevine operating here.'

Williams nodded gloomily. He looked a different man, somehow smaller, somehow older.

'You must think me a real bastard,' he said quietly.

236

'Come again?' said Blizzard.

'It must seem to you that all I am interested in is the money.'

'The thought had crossed my mind.'

'Look,' said the administrator, face lined and drawn. 'Let me level with you. This hospital is in deep financial trouble. We've managed to keep it quiet, but if this Harry Josephs thing gets out, the Press will be all over this place like a rash.'

'How deep is the trouble?' asked the inspector.

'Eight and a half million,' said the administrator bleakly. 'That's why tomorrow's decision is so important. With a bit of creative accounting, I should be able to avoid redundancies among the staff.'

'How many?' asked Blizzard. 'How many would go?'

'Sixty, seventy maybe,' shrugged Williams. 'Mostly back-office people but I might have to make some nursing staff redundant.'

'Starting with the older ones, I assume?' asked Blizzard, thinking of Maureen Cox.

'Yes.' Williams gave a dark laugh. 'Who needs those coming to the end of their careers, eh, Inspector?'

Blizzard nodded gloomily. He'd heard the chief constable make the same arguments in several budget meetings.

'Be honest with me,' said Williams. 'Do you suspect one of my nursing staff of killing the old man?'

'I really have no idea.'

'Have you considered the possibility that one of the patients could have done it?'

Blizzard stared at him.

'Some of them get pretty disturbed,' continued Williams. 'Especially at night. It's one of the things with dementia, and when they're like that, they don't know what they're doing half the time. Wouldn't be the first time something like this has happened in a hospital. I used to be deputy administrator at a unit for the elderly in London and we had at least two patients kill each other. The last one gave an old man bleach to drink. Thought it was Hansa Lager.'

'Easy mistake to make,' said Blizzard.

Before either of them could speak, the office door opened and in walked the young security guard Keegan Rymes.

'The nurses want to know if they can go back in the room,' he said, looking at Blizzard. 'One or two of the patients have woken up and are getting restless what with them just wheeling the old fella out.'

Blizzard glanced at Colley.

'Go and have a word with the sister, will you?' he said.

The sergeant disappeared into the corridor.

'So what do you think?' asked Rymes.

Blizzard looked at him.

'I'm sorry?' he said.

'What do you reckon's happened? The nurses said it looks suspicious. What do you want me to do?'

'I don't want you to do anything, son,' said the inspector. 'We're going to finish up here then leave a couple of uniformed officers on the ward for the next few hours. They'll handle whatever needs doing.'

'Surely there's something for me to do.'

'Might I suggest you go back to your office and do what you normally do,' said Blizzard. 'Make a cup of tea and finish the crossword.'

'Actually,' said Rymes as Colley walked back into the room, 'I'd quite like to hang around here, see if I can be of use.'

'Just go back to your office,' said Williams, noticing the inspector's growing irritation. He gave the guard a reassuring nod. 'Thank you for your help. I am sure the officers will get in touch with you if they need anything else.'

Rymes looked for a moment as if he was about to protest, but thought better of it, turned and left the room.

'I'll leave you to it as well,' said Williams, standing up.

Blizzard nodded and the administrator

followed his security guard out into the corridor. When they had gone, the inspector looked at Colley.

'What you thinking?' asked the sergeant.

'I'm thinking that no one is a suspect and everyone is a suspect, David.'

'Including the patients?' asked the sergeant.

'Meaning?'

'Not sure you'll like it.'

'Whatever you say, I will listen to it in my usual magnanimous fashion.'

'Yeah, that's what worries me,' said the sergeant. 'OK, here goes. If you take Maureen Cox out of the equation because she had clocked off, the only person left on the ward whom we know dislikes Harry Josephs, is George Moore. You heard what Williams said — sometimes they don't know what they're doing, especially at night.'

He paused but there was no reaction from Blizzard.

'So, *if* Josephs was smothered, and Reynolds is right that it would not take much force to do it . . . '

The sergeant did not complete the sentence but instead watched the inspector to see how his comment had been received. To his relief, Blizzard nodded.

'Yeah,' said the inspector, standing up. 'Yeah, you're right. Of course, there is another striking fact about all of this, one which we have rather overlooked. If we assume that George is right about the night Desmond Fairley was gunned down, and that Bates or Josephs, or possibly both of them, helped set it up . . . '

'Then both have died within twenty-four hours.'

'Exactly,' said Blizzard, opening the door. 'And that particular road leads to one Morris Raynor, the man we know will do anything to stop being sent back to prison. Now isn't that interesting?'

Walking out into the nurses' station, the inspector was confronted by a uniformed officer who had pushed his way through the gathering of staff.

'Sorry, sir,' he said, 'but thought you would like to know. There's a bloke been brought into the A & E. He was found with gunshot wounds. They reckon he'll die.'

'No,' said Blizzard. 'I wouldn't like to know.'

21

Maureen Cox stared across the breakfast table at her husband, who was partially concealed by the morning newspaper.

'He's dead,' she said quietly.

Her husband lowered the newspaper.

'Who's dead?' he asked.

'Harry Josephs. He's dead.'

Vic Cox said nothing and went back to his newspaper.

★　★　★

After grabbing a couple of hours of sleep, a weary John Blizzard walked into the side room on Ward 46 and watched as the nursing staff helped George Moore out of his bed and into a wheelchair. He was the last to go and all the other beds in the room were empty. Graham Ross and a fellow forensics officer were already standing in the corridor, ready to move in when the room had been vacated.

As one of the nurses pushed him towards Blizzard, George looked up at the inspector.

'They tell me he's dead,' he said, eyes

bright. 'Harry Josephs. Is it true? Is he dead, John?'

Blizzard nodded.

'He's dead,' he said.

'I told you,' said George, a hint of triumph in his voice. 'I bloody well told you. You'll have to launch an investigation now. You'll bloody well have to.'

Blizzard watched pensively as the nurse wheeled his friend out into the corridor.

'Yes,' murmured the inspector, 'I guess we will.'

★ ★ ★

The hitman stared across the breakfast table at Morrie Raynor, who was partially concealed by the morning newspaper.

'He's dead,' said the man.

Morrie Raynor lowered the newspaper.

'You found out who he's been talking to?' he said.

'I have a pretty good idea. Caught a glimpse of him last night.'

'Then sort it.'

And Morrie Raynor went back to his newspaper.

★ ★ ★

The principal of Queen Mary's eyed Colley uneasily as the two men sat in his office at the college shortly after 8.30. Outside, they could hear the sound of the first students arriving.

'What is this about?' asked Brian Morton, uneasily surveying the sergeant's grim demeanour. 'I really am rather busy.'

'Revising for your next pub quiz?' The sergeant did even try to conceal his distaste for the man.

'No,' said the principal icily. 'I have a governors' meeting this afternoon and I need to prepare my report. They will want an update on this terrible business. It is doing awful damage to the reputation of this college.'

'I imagine they want to know why you keep losing students. Well, you can tell them that two more teenagers were taken ill overnight. And guess what? They both turn out to be your students. What are you going to do, expunge them as well?'

'Jesus,' said Morton, burying his head in his hands, 'this is awful. How are they?'

'Do you know, that is the first time you have seemed genuinely concerned about the welfare of your students.'

Morton did not say anything.

'They got lucky,' said the sergeant, 'but we really do need to bring this to an end before we have any more deaths.'

Morton nodded. All the fight seemed to have drained from him.

'How can I help?' he asked.

'Information on another of your ex-students.'

'I thought you'd decided that Amy Reddington was responsible?'

'She's not the only one we're looking at,' said Colley, as Heather Morrison walked in, clutching a folder. 'Well?'

'Empty,' she said.

'What's empty?' asked Morton anxiously.

'I knew I had seen the name before,' said Colley, 'then it hit me. I saw it last night — on one of your files.'

'Who exactly are we talking about?' asked Morton uneasily.

Colley took the file from Heather and placed it on the desk. Brian Morton read it and closed his eyes.

★   ★   ★

Shortly after 8.30, Blizzard was sitting in his office, eyes closed as he battled against the thick-headed feeling that comes with too much alcohol and too little sleep, when he heard someone walk into the room. He opened his eyes to see Arthur Ronald.

'So,' said the superintendent, sitting down heavily, 'George Moore was right. Old Harry

Josephs was in danger, after all.'

'Not sure really,' said Blizzard, reaching for his mug of tea and discovering it to be cold. He stood up and went over to the kettle. 'Cuppa?'

'Er, yes, thanks. Assuming it does turn out to be dodgy, you fancy anyone for it?'

'Too many.'

'Meaning?'

'Meaning there were nine nurses on duty at the time he died,' said Blizzard, busying himself at the kettle. 'Not to mention a distinctly over-eager security guard fresh out of kindergarten. Then there's the patients, of course.'

'Yes, but surely you don't fancy one of them for this?' asked Ronald.

'Just one.'

'And who,' said Ronald quietly, 'might that be?'

'I think we both know the answer to that one, Arthur. Then, of course, there is our friend Morrie Raynor. If he had convinced himself that Harry was going to spill the beans about the murder of Fairley, or perhaps his latest drugs venture, that would make a pretty strong motive to have him killed. We're checking if any of the nurses have received unexplained payments in recent days.'

There was silence in the room for a few moments, apart from the noise of the inspector making the tea. He had just set the mugs down on the desk when, without knocking on the office door, Peter Reynolds walked in. Both officers eyed him with surprise; the pathologist had never, to their knowledge, visited Abbey Road Police Station.

'Bloody hell, we are honoured,' said the inspector. 'What brings you here?'

'What happened at the hospital has been troubling me,' said the pathologist sitting down. 'I can't get it out of my mind.'

'Welcome to my world,' murmured Blizzard.

'I think what worries me most is the idea that you suspect Maureen Cox.'

'Not closing ranks on me, are you?' said Blizzard, slyly.

Reynolds ignored the comment and placed a piece of paper on the desk.

'So I pulled a favour,' he said. 'You know I wanted to make sure that the old man had not been poisoned? Well, I got a friend of mine out of bed to do a rush job on the samples I took last night. I know you are somewhat scathing about the golf club, Blizzard, but it does come in handy sometimes.'

Blizzard's time to ignore the comment.

'And what did the results show?' he asked instead.

'That whatever killed Harry Josephs, it was not that. Not unless he was poisoned by leek and potato pie — and even given the abominable nature of the food at the hospital, I am pretty sure it would not be fatal.'

'He could still have been smothered, though,' said Blizzard, looking at the pathologist for affirmation. 'I mean, we can't rule that out, can we?'

'Not until I do the post-mortem.' Reynolds stood up and made to leave. 'But I wouldn't get your hopes up, Blizzard, I really wouldn't. If you ask me, this is another old man passing away in the middle of the night and nothing to do with Maureen Cox.'

Once he had left the room, Ronald also stood up.

'Like I have said all along,' he said. 'Unless we hear anything to the contrary, this really has to take a back burner. I understand you had a fatal shooting last night and two other kids taken ill. That's more important.'

'I guess so,' said Blizzard wearily.

Once the superintendent had left the room, Blizzard scanned a couple of reports, resolving to head for the CID room after reading them, but the night's exertions caught up with him and he found himself snoozing until his slumber was disturbed by a knock on the door.

'Can't a man get any sodding sleep round here?' asked the inspector grumpily, as Colley walked into the room. 'And how come you look so bloody bright-eyed and bushy-tailed?'

'Had three hours' sleep,' said the sergeant.

'That's good.'

'Doesn't sound good to me,' grunted Blizzard.

'Ah, you wait 'til young Fee presents you with a bouncing baby Blizzard.'

'Don't,' winced the inspector. 'Have you been to the college yet? Did they confirm it?'

'Oh, aye. I knew I'd seen it somewhere — it's an unusual name — but then we came across Amy Reddington's empty folder and were distracted. Here, look at this.'

Blizzard peered at the scrawl as the sergeant produced a piece of paper from his jacket pocket and placed it on the desk.

'Your handwriting is crap,' said the inspector.

'Then let me translate,' beamed the sergeant. 'That's a note of what the principal just told me. It just so happens that our friend Keegan Rymes used to go to Queen Mary's College but, like his girlfriend Amy Reddington, was kicked out for supplying drugs to other students. Happened three years ago. It was just about the first decision that the principal took when he came into the job. It was the start of the Great Expunging.'

'Eh?'

'Never mind. What's more important is that we know we're looking in the right direction. So, I did a bit of checking through our records, like you suggested, and guess what? Chummy's got a youth court conviction for selling cannabis to a couple of teenagers in a playground over on the east side. Got a slapped wrist and told not to do it again.'

'Somehow I don't think that worked. You talk to the security guy at the hospital about him?'

'Yeah, just come off the phone to him. Turns out he has had his suspicions about Keegan Rymes for a while.'

'Suspicions about what?' asked Blizzard. 'Drugs?'

'Oddly, no. Some money went missing from an old dear who fell on one of the wards and Rymes was the first to help her. Afterward, she complained that a tenner had gone out of her dressing-gown pocket. There had been other similar incidents, but the security guy couldn't prove anything. However, he did start to keep him under surveillance.'

'And?'

'Turns out the kid has been hanging about the pharmacy more than is necessary for his job. There's a CCTV camera at the end of the corridor. The security guy is bringing the films in, but reckons they show that Rymes met a bloke called Martin Goddard on at least eleven occasions — he's an assistant to one of the pharmacists. Mid-twenties, not been there long. At first, the security guy assumed they were having a crafty smoke but after a while he started to wonder if there was more to it.'

'Do we know anything about this Goddard bloke?'

'Unfortunately, yes.'

'Unfortunately?'

'Yeah,' said Colley. 'You know when Heather said she had checked everyone at the pharmacy and that they had all come up clean? Well, she missed something.'

Blizzard closed his eyes.

'Arthur will love this,' he groaned.

'Love what?' asked the superintendent, walking back into the room.

'Oops,' said the sergeant.

Blizzard sighed.

'Well?' said Ronald, looking at Colley.

'It seems,' said the sergeant, 'that in our initial checks on the hospital pharmacy,

251

something slipped through a crack.'

'See, that's why I am so keen on properly maintained paperwork,' said the superintendent, staring pointedly at Blizzard's overflowing in-tray. 'You just can't be too careful.'

'Not sure it was Heather's fault, mind,' said the sergeant. 'Some bright spark had filed it in the wrong place, which explains why we didn't flag anything up when the hospital asked us to security check him before he got the job there.'

'I take it that our friend Goddard has a guilty secret as well?' asked Blizzard bleakly.

'Oh, aye. Turns out we were called into his former place of employment three years ago but it was marked n.f.a. Stuff had been going missing but nothing could be proved.'

'Don't tell me,' said Blizzard, 'he worked at a pharmacy?'

'Down on Ranson Street,' nodded the sergeant. 'Care to guess what he had been suspected of nicking?'

'Throat lozenges.'

'Hardly.' Colley hesitated for dramatic effect. 'Methodone. Heather put a call into the chemists a few minute ago — the manager confirmed it all.'

'Time to have him in for a chat, I think,' said Blizzard, glancing at Ronald, who nodded. 'Bring him in, will you, David? Oh, and get Keegan Rymes in as well. I'll show the little bastard that we can run an investigation without his help.'

'Well ahead of you, guv. And Amy Reddington? Do we bring her in?'

Blizzard hesitated.

'Guv?' said the sergeant.

'I'm thinking,' said the inspector, conjuring up an image of the canteen assistant's cheerful smile.

'I mean,' said Colley, selecting his words carefully, 'she is Keegan Rymes's girlfriend. We've checked and she's on days today. Be easy to pick her up. You want me to go?'

'No, I'll do it,' said Blizzard heavily. 'Shit, I can't. My car's still at Heslington.'

'Ahead of you on that one as well. I've got traffic bringing it in now.' Colley glanced at his watch. 'Should be here, I reckon.'

'You're a good lad.' Blizzard stood up and reached for his jacket from the back of the chair. 'You get Rymes and Goddard and I'll sort the girl. How's Ramsey doing with the shooting?'

'Apparently, they're having trouble finding an ID for the guy.'

As the officers walked into the corridor, the DCI's mobile phone rang. He fished it out of the pocket.

'Blizzard,' he said.

'Mather,' said the voice at the other end. He sounded shaken. 'You know you said it might be time to come in?'

'What's happened, Alex?'

'That shooting on your patch last night. Turns out the vic is the informant who was feeding me information on Morrie Raynor. Lad called Jamie. I reckon I could be next.'

'Jesus, Alex.'

'I know, I know,' said Mather. 'I'm getting out of here, but there's one thing you need to know first. See, not long before he died, Jamie told me something really interesting . . . '

Three minutes later, Blizzard pressed the cancel button on his phone and turned to the others.

'Bingo,' he beamed.

22

John Blizzard walked with heavy step into the canteen at Hafton General Hospital. Approaching the counter, he was greeted by a pleasant smile from Amy Reddington.

'Hiya,' she said, turning to the woman standing next to her. 'Carol, this is the policeman I told you about. We've got quite . . . '

Her voice tailed off as she saw the expression on Blizzard's face.

'What's wrong?' she said.

'Sorry, Amy,' said Blizzard, 'but I am arresting you on suspicion of conspiracy to supply drugs.'

'See,' said Amy, turning to Carol again, 'you never can trust them.'

★   ★   ★

Alex Mather took a final look round the living room of his damp first floor flat and gave a slight smile. He would not miss the place. Whatever the future held, he would not miss the place. Shouldering his bag and reaching down to pick his keys off the wooden coffee table, he headed out into the hallway, tensing

255

when he saw the figure of a man silhouetted through the glass in the front door.

'Shit,' hissed the detective and turned back into the living room.

Seconds later, the front door was kicked in with a tearing of wood and shattering of glass. The intruder barged his way into the living room. He stood and stared at the open window with the curtain fluttering in the breeze. Alex Mather's time as an undercover detective was at an end.

★ ★ ★

'Come on,' said Blizzard irritably. 'Don't muck me around, son. We know what you've been up to.'

He and Colley were in one of the interview rooms at Abbey Road Police Station, staring across the table at Keegan Rymes, who was sitting next to Martin Goddard, a sallow, dark-haired man. His metal-rimmed spectacles give him a studious look and he sat in silence, his demeanour calm and collected, unlike Rymes, who fidgeted constantly.

'But I'm telling you, we ain't done nothing wrong,' said the security guard.

'That remains to be seen,' replied Blizzard. 'Turns out your gaffer reckons you might be nicking stuff. Money.'

Rymes seemed to relax slightly.

'Oh,' he said, 'is that what all this is about?'

'Is it true?' asked Blizzard. The change in demeanour was not lost on the inspector. 'A bit of a tea leaf, are we?'

'If I hold my hands up to it, can I go?' A cunning look had crossed the security guard's face.

'We'll see.'

'Then yeah, yeah, I did nick some cash.'

'Why?'

'They had no need of it. They were really old anyway.'

'And as such deserved some respect,' said Blizzard sharply.

'Look, I'm holding my hands up to it, what more do you want?' Rymes seemed to be growing in confidence. 'So I nicked money from a couple of wrinklies, ain't exactly the worst crime in the world.'

'You steal from Harry Josephs?' asked Blizzard.

'Now come on,' said Rymes quickly. 'I took cash from an old girl as fell outside Ward 16 and another one in Ward 34 but I ain't done nowt like that in Ward 46. Honest.'

Blizzard glanced at his sergeant.

'What do we think?' he asked. 'Do we believe him?'

'Sounds plausible, I guess.'

Rymes relaxed again.

'All this is very interesting,' said Goddard, 'but would you care to tell me why I am here?'

'Ah, yes,' said Blizzard. 'Mr Goddard. You're not a thief, are you, Martin? Drugs, that's more your game, I think.'

A slight expression of unease flickered over Goddard's face, the first time they had seen him exhibit any emotion since walking into the room.

'We ain't into drugs,' protested Rymes.

Blizzard noticed that he was sweating profusely, the beads glistening on his brow. The inspector smiled slightly; he liked it when they started to sweat.

'Ah, but I think you are, Keegan. How about we start with the deaths of Charlotte Grayson and Bobby Leyton? Oh, and maybe we can throw in Lorraine Hennessey as well. And the other two kids who were brought in here last night. How about that?'

Rymes went pale.

'Time to start telling the truth, son,' said Blizzard.

Rymes glanced at Goddard, who shrugged. Both of them knew that the game was up. Half an hour later, Blizzard and his sergeant walked out into the corridor.

'And that,' beamed Blizzard, 'is how my generation does it.'

* * *

'This grieves me more than you can know,' said Blizzard, looking across the interview table at Amy Reddington.

The inspector and Colley were sitting at the same desk on which Goddard and Rymes had signed statements a few minutes earlier and the air in the small room was humid and laden with their sweat.

'I assume,' continued Blizzard, 'that you volunteered the information about you being kicked out of the college so that when we found out for ourselves we had you down for being honest?'

'Something like that,' she said.

Blizzard shook his head.

'What I don't understand,' he said, 'is why you did it. I mean, you're such a bright kid. Why ruin it like this?'

Amy shrugged.

'Always been silly like that, I guess,' she said.

'I'll need more than that.'

'Have you met my father?'

The question surprised the inspector and he shook his head.

'If you had, you'd maybe understand why I did it.' She sounded bitter. 'My father, he always said I was a disappointment. That I had let him down.'

'How old were you when he said that?' said Colley, speaking for the first time in the interview.

'Fourteen, I think. Maybe thirteen, I'm not sure.'

'That's not on.' Colley noticed the inspector looking oddly at him. 'Well, it's not, guv. You have to encourage them, especially at that age.'

'Encourage me, that's a laugh,' said Amy. 'I've got a sister, did you know that? Older than me, heading for a first at Oxford. God knows how she'll get her mortar board on over her halo. Then there's me, a waitress in a hospital canteen. Which one do you think my father cares more about?'

The comment was laced with anger, the first time Blizzard had seen her react in that way.

'But why sell drugs?' asked the inspector. 'I mean, you're hardly going to impress him doing that, are you now?'

'Started as a bit of pocket money,' she said. 'A bit of fun. No one getting hurt. I mean, it was only weed at first. It was only when we tried the other stuff that things went wrong.'

'Lorraine Hennessey a customer?' asked Blizzard.

'Yeah. Said she wanted something stronger.'

'You sell it to her yourself?'

'No. No, there was this lad.'

'Called Malky, I imagine?'

She looked at him in amazement.

'How did you know that?'

'Call it the experience that comes with age, Amy. Tell me about him. We're struggling to track him down.'

She hesitated.

'We'll find him eventually,' said Blizzard.

'His real name is Malcolm. Malcolm Rodgers. Lives over on Rivergarth Avenue. I had a fling with him when I was much younger.' She gave a slight smile. 'I think I only did it to spite my father — Malky was not exactly his idea of the perfect catch.'

'Who mixed up the drugs?' asked Colley.

'Malky.'

'Then Lorraine took ill?' said Blizzard.

'Then Lorraine took ill,' she nodded sadly. 'We never meant that to happen, you have to believe me. It was the first time we had used the stuff and none of the other kids had problems. When Lorraine became ill, we stopped doing it. Got scared. Kept thinking that one day that DI Morrison woman would come knocking on the door, but she never did.'

'So you went back to your old ways?'

'Only weed — and only at the college.

Didn't think it could do any harm. Silly really.'

'But why go back to selling drugs at all?' asked Blizzard. 'I mean, after what happened?'

'Money.' She gave a mirthless laugh. 'I wonder how many times you have heard that one? It's always money, isn't it? When I got kicked out of college, my dad was furious. I've never seen him so mad. Said he was disowning me. Kicked me out of the house. Said I had brought shame on the family and he would never speak to me again.'

'Whatever happened to unconditional love?' murmured Colley.

'Ha, that's a laugh. My dad's love has so many strings you could strangle yourself with them.' She looked at Blizzard. 'What have the others said?'

'Pretty much confirmed what you have told us,' said the inspector. 'What I don't understand, is why go back to the methadone. Why take the risk, Amy? You saw what it did to Lorraine.'

'I didn't go back at first. I stayed clear of it. I told Keegan to do the same thing but he wouldn't listen. Said it would be all right. Malky had said the mix was wrong last time and said it would be safer this time.' She gave a hollow laugh. 'That went well, didn't it?'

'And the drugs?' asked Colley. 'They came from the hospital pharmacy via Martin Goddard, yes?'

'Yes. Martin covered it up on the stock records and Keegan smuggled the stuff out of the building. I think there might have been stuff coming from other hospitals as well. Keegan mentioned Leeds and Nottingham.' She paused and shook her head. 'I guess we're all culpable.'

'Culpable could be the word,' said Blizzard.

'Will we be charged with murder?'

'Or manslaughter. However, if you decided that you wanted to help us . . . ' Blizzard let the words hang in the air. He walked over to lean on the wall.

'Help you how?' she asked uneasily.

'Meaning I don't see why a young kid like you should take the rap for someone else. But if you persist in covering things up, I really am not sure we can help you.'

'I've already told you what I know.'

'Have you? Have you really?' The inspector returned to sit at the table. 'See, I think the idea of going back to selling methadone came from Martin. What do you think?'

'So what if it was?' The answer was cagy.

'He's married, I think,' said Blizzard. 'Got married last year, I believe.'

'I wouldn't know anything about that,' said

Amy, in a flat voice.

'Ah, but I think you do.' Blizzard's voice was harsh now. 'See, we tracked down his wedding certificate: 19th September last year. Big bash, over at The Helm House Hotel. Nice girl, by the sounds of it. What was her name again?'

'Wendy,' said Amy quietly. 'She's called Wendy.'

'I don't suppose you happen to know her maiden name.'

Amy Reddington turned dark eyes on the inspector.

'Raynor,' she said quietly. 'Wendy's name was Raynor.'

Blizzard gave a small smile.

'Was it indeed?' he said.

Amy Reddington started to cry and the detectives said nothing for a few moments.

'Amy,' said Blizzard eventually, reaching out and touching her hand.

She looked up at him, her face rivered with tears.

'Should I tell you what I think?' said Blizzard. 'I think it all started again because Morrie Raynor wanted it to. Saw it as his way of getting back into the drugs market. Is that right?'

'I didn't want to do it,' she said, her voice little more than a whisper. 'None of us

264

wanted to, not even Martin, but Morrie . . . do you know what he's like, Inspector?'

'I do,' nodded Blizzard, squeezing her hand. 'I do indeed, Amy.'

There was silence for a few moments then Amy looked at him, her eyes dark and haunted.

'There's something else you don't know,' she said, in a voice little more than a whisper. 'My last secret.'

Ten minutes later, Blizzard and Colley walked out into the corridor and the inspector leaned with his back against the wall and closed his eyes. Before either of them could speak, Ramsey walked along the corridor.

'You look knackered,' he said the DCI.

'What you got?'

'Reynolds has been on. He's done the PM and there's absolutely nothing to suggest that Harry Josephs died of anything other than natural causes. I guess that puts Maureen Cox in the clear.'

'Guess so,' said Blizzard with a slight smile. 'Best let the old bastard rest in peace, eh?'

'I thought you'd be hacked off,' said Ramsey.

'Ah, well, you thought wrong, Chris. See, it means I don't have to arrest George Moore. That *would* fuel his ideas of a conspiracy.'

'Guv?'

'Never mind. What was the other thing you wanted to talk about?'

'Front counter have been on. There's a bloke demanding to see you. Claims to be Alex Mather. They're a bit dubious that it's him. So am I, to be honest — I had a peep and he looks more like a vagrant. Anyway, he says it's important.'

'It'll be about getting him some shaving gear,' said Blizzard.

'Guv?'

'It can be a life-changing experience, can a shave,' said the DCI and he walked down the corridor with a spring in his step. 'It can do wonders can a shave. I've always thought it.'

'You know,' said Ramsey as he watched the inspector go, 'I'm not sure I will never understand that man.'

'I stopped trying a long time ago,' said Colley. 'A long, long time ago.'

Blizzard sat in the interview room across from the main reception and looked at the bedraggled figure of Alex Mather, the undercover detective's hair lank and matted, his beard unkempt, his cheek swollen and bruised. In the confines of the small room, Blizzard was aware of a rank smell and wondered when Mather had last had a shower.

'Is it over?' asked the inspector.

Mather nodded.

'You were right,' he said. 'Every man has his limits.'

'What made your mind up for you? The shooting last night?'

'Yeah,' nodded Mather. 'See, I made a mistake. Underestimated Morrie Raynor, never thought he would come after me. When you start making mistakes like that, it's time to get out.'

Blizzard's mind went back to Lorraine Hennessey asleep in her hospital bed.

'You might just be right,' he said.

* * *

The exertions of the day, coupled with a lack of sleep, finally caught up with Blizzard and he went home to catch a few hours before the events to come later that night. The inspector was asleep within minutes of his head hitting the pillow. He was woken by a gentle shaking of the shoulder. For a few moments, he was uncertain where he was, but gradually he realized that the figure above him was Fee, illuminated by the light filtering in from the landing.

'What time is it?' he mumbled.

'Half nine.'

'Already?' said Blizzard, sitting up and running a hand across his eyes. 'Bye, I could have slept for hours.'

'I know, same here. Need my rest now.'

He looked at her.

'Something you are not telling me?' he said.

She reached over and snapped on the bedside light then moved back to sit next to him. He noticed that she was holding a small white object. Blizzard stared at it for a few moments.

'Is what I think it is?' he asked.

Fee gave a smile.

'Certainly is.'

23

'You ready for this?' said Colley, glancing at the inspector.

'As ready as I can be,' nodded Blizzard, looking at his sergeant with eyes that gleamed in a darkness only permeated by the light from the dashboard; the inspector had the ignition on and the Granada's heater running.

They were parked on a quiet tree-lined country lane to the east of the city. The officers had arrived shortly before eleven, neither officer speaking as Blizzard drove, each alone with their thoughts. Now parked up half a mile from the northern edge of Heslington village, the inspector glanced in his rear-view mirror as several police vans pulled up behind him. Colley turned round in his seat, squinting through the half light as headlights were dimmed.

'The cavalry are here,' he said. A green Audi edged its way past the vans and pulled up just in front of the Granada. 'That Randall?'

'Yeah. Must be a stoppyback at the Otter and Fish.'

Colley gave a low laugh. He noticed a couple of patrol cars pulling into the road.

'Armed boys are here,' he said.

'Surely I have not become that decrepit yet.'

'That's not 'til Wednesday,' said the sergeant. 'Besides, I've got this horrible feeling that you're going to be around for quite a while yet.'

'Bloody hope so,' said Blizzard.

★ ★ ★

A uniformed officer with a holster resting on his hip alighted from one of the cars and walked along the lane towards the Granada. Max Randall also got out of his vehicle and headed in the same direction. Blizzard got out when they arrived.

'Whose arrest is this then?' said the firearms officer.

'DCI trumps rookie DI,' said Blizzard, glancing at Randall.

'Ah, but you're in Eastern's jurisdiction,' replied Randall. 'This is my patch, matey.'

'Make your mind up, girls,' said the firearms officer.

Another car pulled up further down the lane and the officers turned to see a uniformed chief superintendent walking towards them.

'And my divisional commander trumps all,' said Randall triumphantly.

Blizzard noticed that following the commander was Arthur Ronald but decided not to contest the point.

'Whatever,' he said.

'We ready?' asked the divisional commander.

There was the grumble of an engine and everyone turned to watch as a small earth-mover edged its way round the corner and parked behind the last of the police vehicles.

'We are now,' said the firearms officer. 'Thought I'd bring it along in case our friend decides not to open the gate.'

'OK, let's get this thing done,' said the commander. He gave Blizzard a hard look. 'Oh, and remember, this is an Eastern operation. Randall gets the arrest. Understand?'

Blizzard was about to speak but a glance from Ronald silenced him. The inspector satisfied himself with glowering at the commander as he got back into the Granada.

'Bloody stuffed shirts,' he grumbled, starting the car moving.

The inspector led the convoy slowly along the lane until it reached the edge of the village and, with extinguished headlights, pulled up outside a newly built gated housing estate, hidden behind a large stone wall. The officers could vaguely glimpse, through the wrought-iron bars of the gate, a cluster of large detached houses with carefully coiffeured lawns and creeping ivy winding its way elegantly across mock-Elizabethan façades.

'Who says crime doesn't pay?' murmured Colley.

Blizzard got out of his car and, as others converged on the front entrance, he walked over to the gate, where he ran his finger down the brass nameplates before stopping at the final one. He was sorely tempted to press the button, but a sharp look from the approaching Randall changed his mind and Blizzard sighed and pointed it out to the DI. Randall gave the slightest of smiles and pressed.

'Who is it?' said a disembodied voice. Both officers instantly recognized the fluted tones.

'DI Randall from Lowe Street. I want to come in.'

'You got a warrant?'

'Yes.'

'Show me.'

Randall reached into his coat pocket and produced a piece of paper, which he held up to the CCTV camera attached to a tree behind the wall. There was a pause.

'That John Blizzard next to you?' said the voice.

'Yes, but — '

'I'll only talk to Blizzard. Put him on.'

'Hang on, Morrie, I hardly think you're — ' began Randall.

'Put him on.'

Trying to conceal his look of triumph, Blizzard glanced across at the approaching Eastern divisional commander, who in turn looked at Arthur Ronald. Ronald shrugged.

'Your call,' was all he said to the commander.

The commander said nothing and turned away. Blizzard brushed past a glowering Randall and spoke into the intercom.

'I'm here, Morrie,' he said.

'What's this about, Blizzard?'

'Not really prepared to stand in the street discussing it. It's bloody cold and my bad back is feeling it. Neither of us is getting any younger.'

'Are you here to arrest me?'

'Depends how our conversation goes, Morrie.'

'OK, come in,' said Raynor, as the firearms inspector walked up to join Blizzard. 'And come alone — lose the popguns.'

With a dubious expression on his face, the firearms officer looked at the divisional commander.

'I have no idea who the fuck is in charge here,' he said, moving away from the gate and talking in a low voice so that it was not picked up by the intercom, 'but whoever it is, I'm not sure that this is a great idea.'

'Not sure we have any other options,' replied Blizzard, glancing up to the CCTV camera then spotting a second one further along the wall. 'He can see everything we do anyway.'

'I'm not so sure,' said the firearms inspector in a low voice. 'I reckon there's a blind spot, round the side — noticed it as we came in. I reckon we could get a man — '

'No,' said Blizzard sharply. His voice softened as he looked at the firearms inspector. 'Look, I know you mean for the best, but there's no way Morrie Raynor would be stupid enough to try anything with you lot around. If he had wanted to kill me, he would have done it by now — he had his chance before, remember?'

There were a few moments' silence.

'Your call, John,' said Ronald, turning to look at the Eastern divisional commander, who nodded. 'Got to be your call, old son.'

'Less of the old,' said Blizzard and walked over to the intercom.

'I'm coming in,' he said. 'Alone.'

There was no reply from Raynor but, with

a whirring sound, the gate moved gently sideways and Blizzard stepped into the estate. It took him a couple of minutes to walk past several other houses before he reached Raynor's home, which stood in the heart of the estate. The front door was open but there was no one standing on the doorstep. Glancing up at the picture window, Blizzard could see a large staircase, partially illuminated by the light from the street lamp outside the house. For a few moments, he stood there, heart pounding, sweat starting on his brow, gathering his courage. When no one came out, he walked slowly up the drive and into the house. As his eyes became accustomed to the gloom, he could see that he was standing in a spacious tiled hallway at the end of which was the staircase stretching up to what appeared to be an oak gallery. The only sound was the ticking of a grandfather clock standing at the far end of the hall.

'As I recall, it was a similarly dark winter's night last time,' said Raynor's voice from the darkness.

'It was indeed, Morrie, but it feels a long time ago and, like I said, we're both getting too old for this. Why don't you show yourself?'

Blizzard tried to keep his voice calm, but for all his efforts, could not prevent the slight tremble.

'Scared?' said the voice.

The voice came from above him and Blizzard looked up at the gallery. As he did so, he noticed movement at the top of the stairs and a figure stepped forward from the shadows and stood motionless, eyeing him silently.

'That's better,' said Blizzard, taking a step forward.

'Stay where you are!'

Blizzard stopped.

'Just stay where you are,' repeated Raynor, 'and tell me what you want from me.'

'Where do I start? Des Fairley, maybe? I know you had him killed.'

'Ancient history,' snorted Raynor. The tone of his voice became mocking. 'All ancient history. Besides, I'd like to see you prove anything. No one else ever did, not even your big buddy George Moore. How is he? Still away with the fairies?'

'Then there's the little matter of the shooting of a police informant over on the Howgill Estate last night. I'm pretty sure that was done at your behest as well.'

Raynor remained motionless at the top of the stairs.

'You're fishing, Inspector,' he said, his voice sounding strong and confident. 'Just like all the others — it's all guesswork.'

'We've lifted your son-in-law. Did you know that?'

'So I heard. Why do you want him?'

'Come on, Morrie. I think you know the answer to that one. We want to ask him a few questions about a couple of dead teenagers.'

'What's that got do with me?' For the first time, Morrie Rayor's voice sounded a little uncertain.

'We can link their deaths back to drugs supplied by your son-on-law. He's in a whole bucketload of trouble.'

'So? It's nothing to do with me,' snorted Raynor. 'So my son-in-law has done something stupid, so what? You can't pin anything on me and you know it.'

'Not what I'm hearing. See, we've lifted some of your little friends, Morrie. Amazing what folks will say when they face the prospect of a long stretch inside. What about you? You fancy going back inside?'

'You're bluffing.'

'We've got you, Morrie,' said Blizzard quietly. 'We really have.'

There was silence for a few moments.

'I can't go back,' said Raynor. His voice sounded small and . . . and . . . Blizzard tried to come up with the word. Old, that was it, Morrie Raynor sounded old.

'And I haven't even started talking about

the murder of Geoff Bates yet. Give me enough time and I reckon I can get that one to stick as well.'

'That was not down to me.' The words came quicker than the others.

'Well, whether it was or it wasn't, it doesn't really matter, does it? You're going away for something out of all this. The game's up.'

'For who, though?'

The voice had regained its composure and Blizzard watched as Morrie Raynor walked down the top four steps so that he was better illuminated by light coming from the street lamp outside the front of the house.

'For who?' repeated Raynor.

The inspector noticed that he had produced a handgun from his coat pocket.

'I'm not going back to prison.' Raynor gave a thin smile.

'Like you said, I should have put a bullet in your brain last time. And you know me, Blizzard, I've always done what the police say. Law-abiding man, me.'

'Come on, Morrie,' said Blizzard, heart pounding, hands clammy. 'Even if you kill me, you can't escape — we've got the place surrounded by armed officers.'

'Then we'll walk right through them.'

'It didn't work last time and it won't work this time.'

Raynor slowly and deliberately raised the handgun to point at the inspector.

'It would seem then,' he said quietly, 'that we have run out of options, my dear inspector.'

The single shot rang out in the darkness of the night.

24

'W*ould* he have shot you?' asked Colley, as
the inspector brought the Granada to a halt
in the carpark next to the allotments early the
next afternoon.

Blizzard turned off the ignition and turned
in his seat to look at the sergeant. It was
the first time they had really talked about the
incident.

'Who knows?' he shrugged.

'The armed officer seemed pretty certain,'
said the sergeant. 'Said he had no option but
to shoot the moment he saw Raynor point his
gun at you.'

'I guess the inquiry will have to decide on
that,' said the inspector, as the officers got out
of the car. 'What matters is that he's dead.
Not sure many people will mourn him. From
what I hear, our lot are too busy arguing
about who should take responsibility. Now
he's dead, they can't run fast enough in the
other direction!'

'Any closer to the guy who shot Mather's
informant?' asked Colley, as the two men got
out of the car.

'Just a first name. Raynor's death seems to

have loosened tongues. Turns out he's an ex-pat living in Spain. Sounds like he was the one who did Fairley and there're suggestions that Morrie asked him to do a couple over in Manchester back in the early Eighties. GMP are checking their records.'

'We going to get him then?'

'Arthur's onto the Foreign Office.' Blizzard grinned. 'Hey, thee and me might get a nice trip to Fuengirola.'

'That'd be nice, bit of sunshine.' There was silence for a few moments then Colley looked across the roof of the car at the inspector with a curious expression on his face. 'What does it feel like? I mean, to have a gun pointed at you like that? What do you think about?'

'I guess I thought about all the things I would lose if he pulled the trigger.'

'Yeah, Fee would be devastated,' nodded the sergeant. He hesitated, suddenly uncomfortable. 'As would I.'

'Thank you.' Blizzard looked up as a green Audi pulled into the car-park, tyres crunching on the gravel. 'Anyway, enough man-bonding.'

'Too right.'

Max Randall parked the Audi next to Blizzard's car and got out.

'How you feeling, matey?' he said, placing a hand on the inspector's shoulder.

'Like a man with the whole of his life ahead of him.'

'What there is of it,' said Randall. 'You're no spring chicken.'

'Yes, thank you, Max,' murmured Blizzard. 'Come on, let's get this done.'

The officers started to walk up the snow-covered path through the allotment.

'Your arrest, eh?' said Blizzard. 'Even if you are on my patch.'

Randall gave him a rueful look. Reaching the top, Blizzard and Randall turned right through one of the gates. Colley stayed on the path. Maureen Cox was standing by the shed, coat collar turned up against the biting chill of the morning. Vic was at the bottom of the allotment, staring out across his winter vegetables.

'Thought we'd find you here,' said Blizzard.

'Is is true?' she asked. 'Is he dead?'

'Morrie's dead,' nodded the inspector.

'The radio said it was an armed police officer who killed him. They said that you were trying to arrest him when it happened.' She looked at him for confirmation.

'All true,' said Blizzard. 'Raynor didn't even know he was there. Neither did I, for that matter.'

'I'm glad he was.'

Blizzard hesitated and something in his demeanour made her look at him.

'But you're not here to tell me about Morrie, are you?' she said.

'I'm afraid not.'

'Surely you still don't think I had anything to do with the death of Harry Josephs? Don't look like that, I heard you were asking questions.'

'No, we are pretty satisfied that was natural causes.'

'Then, what? I am in the clear and you can stop these silly insinuations.'

'I am afraid not, Maureen. This is Detective Inspector Randall from Eastern CID. He's investigating the murder of Geoff Bates.'

Both detectives looked down the allotment at the silent figure of Vic Cox.

'You don't seriously think that he had anything to do with it?' said Maureen, unable to conceal the astonishment from her voice. 'That's even more ridiculous than thinking that I killed Harry Josephs.'

'I would have said the same thing until DI Randall here told me that Bates was shot with an old service revolver. Vic did National Service, I think?'

'After the war. The Middle East.' Maureen looked down the allotment to where her husband was now watching them. 'But surely you don't think he used it to kill Geoff Bates? That's about as crazy as the idea that one of the nurses killed Harry Josephs. You're getting like George.'

'That's what I thought, but if what happened to Lorraine Hennesey taught me anything, it's not to be complacent. Take nothing for granted.' The inspector looked at her. 'I'd just got the wrong old man, hadn't I?'

'I don't know what you're talking about. I really don't.'

'Ah, but I think you do, Maureen. See, DI Randall also told me that Geoff Bates had a new woman in his life. I think you might know her name. You're about the same age.'

Maureen looked at Randall.

'Irene Cloughton,' said the DI.

'So that's how Geoff knew,' breathed Maureen. Her voice became a mixture of disbelief and bitterness. 'She promised on her baby's life. Said she would never tell anyone.'

'And I think you'll find that she kept that promise,' said Blizzard. 'How do you know her?'

'We were once the closest of friends, me and Irene.' She gave a slight smile. 'When the kids were young. We did everything together. Walks round the park, that sort of thing.'

'And, like good friends, I imagine you shared your deepest and darkest secrets?' said Blizzard. 'Tell me about Vic's father.'

Maureen nodded, her expression one of defeat.

'He was a terribly ill man,' she said, pulling her coat tighter around her to keep out the cold. 'Emphysema. Have you ever seen someone suffering from emphysema, Inspector?'

'I know a lot of former railway lads. Seen more of them die than I would care to count.'

'Then you know what agony it is. He suffered, did that man, really suffered. Every day was a nightmare for him.' Tears were close now and she looked down the allotment where Vic was staring at them. 'It was eating Vic up.'

'And the decision to kill him?'

'It was a chance comment that did it.' She gave a mirthless laugh. 'Funny how these things start. Vic said one day that his father would be better dead. I'd not long completed my nurse's training. The rest was easy.'

'How did you do it?'

'Morphine. Easy enough when you know what you're doing. Took him less than five minutes to die. I knew that no one would ask any questions.' She looked at the officers, eyes glistening with tears. 'Was I wrong? I mean, he was finally at peace.'

'It wasn't your decision to make, Maureen,' said Blizzard. 'Why tell Irene about it?'

'I couldn't carry it on my own and Vic refused to talk about it.' She shook her head as if the thought had just struck her. 'Do you know, we have never talked about it. Can you believe that? It was like it never happened. Irene was wonderful, listened to me pour my heart out. And she was as good as her word — kept the secret for years.' Her voice turned bitter again. 'At least I thought she had.'

'Did you know she had taken up with Geoff?' asked Randall.

'No, we drifted apart after the kids grew up. We hadn't seen each other for years. But I never thought she would tell anyone our secret.'

'Well, like I say,' said Blizzard, 'she didn't. In fact, even when Geoff Bates died she never even thought to mention any of this because she didn't think anyone knew about it. Trouble is, Irene was a habitual diary writer and she'd made a note of what you told her all those years ago.'

'And Geoff found it?' asked Maureen, clapping a hand to her mouth.

'Came across it by accident when getting something out of the attic,' nodded Randall. 'At least that's what we assume happened.

When Blizzard suggested I run your name past Irene, she looked horrified. We went up to the attic and the diary had gone.'

'I take it Geoff had tried to blackmail you?' asked Blizzard.

'He came to us a couple of weeks ago,' she nodded. 'Said he knew what we'd done — wouldn't tell me how he knew — and that he'd go to the police if we didn't pay him money. I told Vic that he couldn't possibly prove it, that he was just trying it on, but he wouldn't listen. Got more and more twisted up about it. Said neither of us could survive prison and that we had to kill him. When I had to kick Geoff out of the ward and saw the look on his face, I knew he was right.'

'But I don't think Vic was the one who killed him, was he, Maureen?' said Blizzard quietly. 'See, Vic's too weak to pull a trigger. You told me that.'

Maureen said nothing and Randall stepped forward.

'Maureen Cox,' he said, 'I am arresting you on suspicion of murder. You do not have to say anything but anything you do say may be taken down and given in evidence.'

'Funny,' she said with a sad smile on her face. 'We never did go to Spain.'

Vic Cox watched in motionless silence as the detectives led his wife through the gate.

25

That evening, Blizzard and George Moore sat in the lounge, staring out at night-time Hafton.

'Nice view, eh?' said George.

Blizzard surveyed the snow-covered roofs and the flickering lights of the cars on the city centre roads.

'You've not mentioned that before,' he said. 'You feeling better then?'

'Lots, thanks. The doctor reckoned I had another infection but that it's gone now. They reckon I'll be out at the weekend.'

They sat in silence for a few more moments.

'I been reading about it in the paper,' said George eventually. 'You got Morrie then. You'll be a real legend now, my boy.'

'But Harry died of natural causes. You know that, yeah?'

'Yeah.' There was a pause. 'I'm sorry, old son. I owe you an apology.'

Blizzard turned to look at his friend in surprise.

'Me? Why?'

'All that stuff about Harry Josephs. I was

convinced that they were here to kill him.'
George shook his head. 'Amazing what illness
can do to the human mind, isn't it? I only
know what I had been saying because that
nice Nurse Ramage told me. I don't
remember any of it.'

'Now you tell me,' murmured Blizzard.

On the way down the stairs, after leaving
his friend, the inspector visited Ward 23 and
walked into Lorraine Hennessey's room. He
stood and looked in silence at the empty bed
for a few moments, turning when a nurse
walked in.

'When did she die?' asked the inspector
quietly.

'They switched her machine off about an
hour ago. Mum's around if you want to talk
to her. She said she was going for a cup of
tea.'

Deep in thought, Blizzard walked into the
canteen. It felt strange without Amy. Jan
Hennessey was sitting at a corner table, cup
of coffee in hand. She looked up when the
inspector approached. Her face was pale and
she had been crying.

'She's gone,' Jan said quietly. 'Lorraine's
gone.'

'I know.' Blizzard sat down. 'I'm sorry, I
really am.'

She did not say anything.

'Where's your husband?' asked the inspector, looking round the room.

'Away on business.' She shot him a mirthless look. 'He's always away on business.'

Blizzard hesitated.

'Look,' he said, 'I know this is not the time, but there is something I really have to talk to you about. You suggested last time that your husband might have been, how can I put it . . . ?'

'Sleeping around?' she said bitterly. 'You can say it.'

'I guess that's what I am trying to say, yes. Look, you know I mentioned a girl called Amy Reddington?'

'The girl you thought had supplied the drugs to Lorraine?'

'We believe that she had an affair with your husband. They met at a career's convention at the college two months after Lorraine was taken ill. We don't think your husband knew what she had done and we think the affair ended just before Christmas. I'm sorry but I thought you needed to know.'

Jan Hennessey stared into her coffee but said nothing.

★   ★   ★

On the short drive back to Abbey Road Police Station, Blizzard noticed a newspaper billboard outside a newsagent. *Hospital receives funding boost*, it said. The inspector allowed himself a smile.

'At least someone is happy,' he murmured.

An hour later, he was sitting in his office, trying to read a report but constantly finding his mind straying to other matters, when there was a light knock on the door.

'Come in,' he said, without looking up from the document.

'Guv?' said a woman's voice.

He looked up to see Heather Morrison. The drugs squad inspector looked nervous and was clutching a white envelope.

'I hear you tracked down Malky,' he said cheerfully and gestured for her to sit.

She remained standing.

'What's that?' he asked, nodding at the envelope.

'My resignation,' she said. 'I made some awful mistakes and three kids are dead because of it.'

Blizzard put down the document he had been reading and picked up the envelope, turning it over in his hands a couple of times before tearing it in two and shying it at his wastepaper basket in the corner of the room.

'But . . . ' she began.

'Heather,' he said, gesturing again for her to sit, which she did this time, 'if every one of us resigned when we made a mistake then there wouldn't be anyone left to run this force. Jesus, take me — I got so wrapped up with the Harry Josephs thing I lost sight of what else was happening. So, resignation refused.'

And Blizzard picked up the document again and started reading. Heather stood up to go.

'Thank you,' she said.

'No problem.'

On her way back to her office, the drugs squad inspector passed Colley in the corridor.

'I still don't understand him,' she said. 'Do you?'

'Who, Blizzard?' grinned the sergeant. 'Na, of course not.'

Colley watched her go, chuckled and headed into the inspector's office.

'You wanted to see me,' said the sergeant.

'Yeah,' said Blizzard, putting the document back in his intray. 'Close the door will you?'

Colley closed the door and Blizzard gestured to the chair.

'Sit down, David,' he said.

'Am I in trouble?' asked the sergeant. 'I'm not sure I like the way this is going.'

'No, you're not in trouble,' said Blizzard as the sergeant sat down. 'You asked me a question earlier today and I was not totally truthful with the answer. You asked me what I thought about when Morrie Raynor pointed that gun at me.'

Colley watched his boss intently.

'There was something else,' said Blizzard.

'You're not going to retire, are you?' said Colley. He looked horrified at the thought.

'What?'

'Everyone reckons you're going to retire, all this talk about getting old.'

'Certainly not! Jesus, I've got far too much to live for.' Blizzard hesitated. 'Look, I know you're not supposed to say anything for twelve weeks but . . . '

A beam spread across Colley's face.

'Brilliant,' he said, 'a playmate for Laura. Wonder if the kid will be as grumpy as you are. Hey, what you like when it comes to Postman Pat?'

John Blizzard tried not to smile — but in the end, it was just too much of an effort.

Other titles published by
The House of Ulverscroft:

TO DIE ALONE

John Dean

When the bodies of a man and his dog are found on the northern hills, Detective Chief Inspector Jack Harris and his team find themselves plunged into a violent world where life counts for little. The team is drawn ever deeper into the machinations of organized crime. Then as the fear grows that a ruthless killer is living in their midst, a second murderous assault rocks the hilltop community of Levton Bridge. As the mystery deepens, and people start to panic, the investigation reveals a disturbing world of secrets, half-truths and betrayals where lives and loves are casualties . . .

THE RAILWAY MAN

John Dean

The opening of a railway museum is marred by the murder of a former railman and Detective Chief Inspector John Blizzard is faced with some awkward truths. It seems that his friends are concealing vital information from him. And soon he discovers that the dead man's legacy is a dark shadow that spreads right across the northern city of Hafton. Finally, John Blizzard has to confront a betrayal that he never thought possible . . .

THE DEAD HILL

John Dean

The discovery of a dead gangland figure in a quarry brings back dark memories for Detective Chief Inspector Jack Harris and the hilltop community in which he works. As the detective investigates the murder, not only is he forced to deal with the hostile villains, frightened townsfolk and colleagues who doubt his capacity to bring the killer to justice, he also has to confront part of his past that he hoped would be forgotten. And in doing so, he is forced to re-evaluate the loyalties of those closest to him.

STRANGE LITTLE GIRL

John Dean

The anniversary of a mother and child's murder brings back painful memories for Detective Chief Inspector John Blizzard and his right-hand man Detective Sergeant Dave Colley. But the murder of the main suspect, whose body is found lying next to the grave of the victims, reopens a case everyone thought was dead. The officers' investigation leads them to a murky and secretive world. But they have a chance to solve, once and for all, one of the greatest mysteries in the city's criminal history . . . and to track down the strange little girl who somehow escaped the slaughter of her mother and sister.